Blind Witness

Blind Witness

Vicki Goldie

Victorina Press
www.victorinapress.com

Typesetting and Layout: Heidi Hurst
Cover design © Fiona Zechmeister

British Library Cataloguing in Publication Data
A catalogue record for this book is available from the
British Library.

ISBN: 978-0-9957547-5-1 (Paperback)

Typeset in 11pt Adobe Garamond Pro
Printed and bound in Great Britain by Charlesworth Press

To Richard thank you for the insight, always.

THE CHARTERS'
MYSTERIES SERIES

This series follows the amateur sleuths Major Alasdair Charters and the Honourable Melissa Charters as they inadvertently muddle their way though many investigations but always arrive at the truth. Alasdair was blinded in the First World War and uses his special skills to gain 'insight' into the crimes. The Honourable Melissa who likes to think she is a Socialist, has a large family and set of friends who always seem run into problems. The books will be set both in England and abroad.

Having a husband who is blind, Vicki likes to explore perceptions about this disability and push the boundaries.

PROLOGUE

He heard the crash. It did not wake him. He seldom slept much at night these days. His mind was taken with memories of the war, all blood and terror. A mind tormented by unacknowledged fears of the present and the future.

The crash was the heavy suit of armour from the entrance hall falling over the body on the Aubusson rug that lay in front of the last embers of the hall fire. The falling suit of armour masked the method of death and, though he heard it as it happened, at the time he had no idea what the sound signified. He opened his eyes, listened and heard a further sound, an obscure sound. It wafted fleetingly like mustard gas across the senses. A sound that caused him to frown, one he could not quite place but knew he should do, if he tried. It was dismissed, as silence pervaded the dark. That last sound did not register in his consciousness then, but it would come to mean the difference between life and death.

The screaming started.

ONE

The New Forest, 1922

FRIDAY EVENING

'Good grief, Alasdair, do you have to be so independent?' Melissa glared at her husband as he continued to struggle with his stiff evening collar and bow tie, muttering under his breath. Softening her voice with affection, she continued, 'Thomas would happily have stayed and helped you. After all, it is his job.'

Alasdair turned towards her voice and scowled. 'I wanted to do it myself.' And then, as if he realised that he sounded like a petulant schoolboy, he added, 'It is just that I still feel so useless.'

Instantly contrite, Melissa crossed the room and hugged him. 'Of course you're not useless. I just wish sometimes you were not so stubborn – you seem determined to make things hard on yourself.'

'It's just I want to get the tie right. I suppose it is a complete mess.'

Standing back, she just could not help admiring the handsome man she loved as he stood in front of her, seemingly unaware of her scrutiny. Still with the air of command about him, even out of uniform and in his tails, crisp white shirt and tie. She looked at the tie critically, 'Well, it is a little crooked; I wish you hadn't sent Thomas away. I won't be much help, haven't the foggiest, I'll have to get him to teach me.'

'Well, do your best for heaven's sake. If anyone else goes down with a crooked tie, it'll be frowned upon, but if I do, it will be poor Alasdair can't even get his tie right.'

Hearing his fear underlying the complaint, Melissa forced herself not to sigh. He hated sighing. 'Oh, Alasdair, that is unfair. They are all, well nearly all, family here. No one is going to be judging you. Why should they? To them you are a war hero – one of the few that came back. We are here for a lovely weekend to be spoiled rotten by Brigadier Ferguson and Aunt Honor. Please try to enjoy yourself.'

'Hmph,' he muttered. 'They may not be judging me, but I will be.' He began pacing the room, reaching out and touching odd pieces of furniture, stopping and occasionally resting his hand and following the grain of the wood. 'This is the same room we had last time?'

'Yes, each time we have been.' She bit her lip, remembering the first time they had visited after the war. Alasdair had been newly returned from St Dunstan's Rehabilitation Centre. The Brigadier, ever the bluff, hale, hearty type had made some appalling gaffes, like asking if he could use a knife and fork. It had not been a success and had not been repeated for nearly a year. She glanced at Alasdair and realised he was waiting for her reply. 'Yes, it is the same room. Aunt Honor thought it would be easier that way, and it is one of the bigger rooms, so we are in luck. A shame it is so full of these Victorian monstrosities.' She patted the doors of the huge wardrobe. A wardrobe, she reflected, that an entire homeless family could have slept in.

A sense of guilt crept over her as she remembered the shabby tenement buildings they had passed and observed from the luxury of their first-class carriage on the train from London to the New Forest. Her uncle, generally known to all as Brigadier Ferguson, had sent his Rolls-Royce to pick them up from the station. With Thomas ensconced in the front with the chauffeur and the bags lashed to the rear, they had travelled in comfort and style. How could she reconcile the grime, smoke and struggle of London with the ease and space (acres of space in fact) at this weekend house party at Pennstone Manor? Pennstone was the home of her mother's sister, Lady Honor, both of them born to privilege, the daughters of an earl. It had been quite a comedown when her aunt had married Reginald Ferguson, a young officer with few social connections. But he had risen high and now was at the centre of their formerly large family, sadly depleted by the war. She shuddered to think how one coped losing all your children over the space of a year.

She walked over to the window and gazed out, giving herself a quiet moment. Alasdair didn't mean to make demands and was overly conscious of the burden he perceived himself to be, but as much as she loved him, it was sometimes waring pandering to his black moods. The window, huge by London standards, looked over the rear of the estate. The gardens displayed a dishevelled elegance as winter approached. Melissa noted in passing that many of the hedges could do with a trim. The main lawn needed a final cut. Beyond the formal gardens was a paddock leading down to, and blending into, the New Forest beyond. The leaves were beginning to turn, red and gold, a beauty that moved her. She gave a mental shrug; she refused to let this despairing mood descend. She was so happy to be here; her aunt and uncle were her favourite rellies and she adored the New Forest. Their visits had been few and far between since the war and after Alasdair's discharge from the army on medical grounds. Still, he had been no slouch himself; his career had been curtailed at the rank of major. He refused to use the honorific and refused to leave their service flat in Bloomsbury. He cut himself off from his former friends, turning any away that came to call. Eventually they all stopped coming. The only people he saw, and then often under sufferance, were their respective families. However, he seemed to like Brigadier Ferguson and Pennstone Manor. This could have been because, even in autumn, it had a peace and tranquillity that eased his mind. Was that why he had surprised her and had not balked at her rather timid suggestion that they came here for a weekend away? Even when she had mentioned (with crossed fingers) that it was a small house party?

He stopped pacing. 'Come on,' he said. 'Let's get this over with and hit the cocktails.'

As they left their room, the sound of raised voices carried down the corridor from their host's suite of rooms at the far end of the wing.

'Oh dear,' Alasdair muttered. 'That doesn't bode well.'

'I think she is cross because Brigadier Ferguson has invited other guests, rather than just family, and she had wanted to keep this weekend less formal and easier for us.'

'Me, you mean.'

'Well, you have turned them down any number of times before.'

He grimaced.

'Alasdair, they are lonely. They have lost their sons.' She swallowed quickly and blinked to hold back the emotion she always felt lurking behind her eyes when she thought of all the war dead. So many she had known. So many she had visited in hospital. Her two Ferguson cousins – so handsome, so vibrant, they seemed to lurk around every corner. What must it be like for their parents?

As if sensing Melissa's change of mood, Alasdair, with his hand tucked firmly into the crook of her arm, leant over and said, 'So tell me, what delightful creation are you wearing tonight?'

'A silver sheath dress, rather slinky, if I say it myself.'

He dropped his hand, ran it over her hip, tracing the delightful curves of the sequins that flowed across the dress, and then he pinged her suspender.

'Mmm, see what you mean, but shall I be fighting off cads all evening?'

Melissa's grin was wasted but her voice carried it. 'Oh no, you look far too dashing to have any chance of competition …'

'Humph,' was the reply but when she sneaked a look, he was smiling. She patted her cropped blonde curls – the colour that had named her. She liked the feel of air on the back of her neck, her earrings skimming her shoulders. After she made sure his hand was tucked through her elbow once more, they reached the head of the stairs.

She paused and muttered 'stairs' in a low voice. In response, Alasdair reached for the banister. Progressing down the stairs, one arm through Melissa's and one on the rail, he descended. The smooth texture of the – no doubt well-polished – banister rail slid like silk under his fingers. The stairs were wide and carpeted (but thankfully not slippery) beneath the soft soles of his patent leather evening shoes. Every few steps he could feel the brass rods that held the carpet in place as his heels threatened to catch on them. Silently, he counted their number.

There was a young man standing at the bottom of the stairs. Melissa watched a play of emotions flit across his face. Was that admiration? They did rather make a handsome couple, she preened. Then his countenance changed to one of astonishment.

'Major Charters? Alasdair? Good grief, man. I thought you were dead.'

TWO

Melissa gently guided Alasdair to the safety of the elegant black and white chequered marble hallway floor and towards the rather scruffy young man who had called up to them. Her eyes quickly took in the ancient suit, the slightly green tinge and the shiny elbows, a dead giveaway of impoverishment. He was young but there were dark shadows under his eyes, early lines about them. Another just-survivor of the war, she surmised. She could see the confusion on his face as he saw no answering recognition on Alasdair's.

'Not dead,' she said, smiling. 'But badly wounded, lost his sight, you'll have to introduce yourself.'

'No need to do that, I'd recognise your voice anywhere, Henry Blake isn't it? Still work for The Times, do you?' Alasdair extended his hand and Henry grasped it firmly.

'Yes, I am still there, plodding away.'

'Hardly. I relish your reports. They are always illuminating.'

'But …?'

'This is my wife, Melissa, long suffering and excellent at reading aloud.'

Melissa had been watching the play of emotions moving over the other man's face; he smiled but it did not quite meet his shadowed eyes. Something was troubling him. Embarrassment, maybe? However, her intuition prompted her to like him. She made a mental note to ask Alasdair about him later. Here, she sensed, was an interesting story.

They wandered into the first drawing room together. Generally, this room was known as the blue drawing room to differentiate it from the second drawing room, known as the green drawing room. An adequate drinks tray was set up on a small mahogany sofa table. The sofa was of a fashionable chintz fabric with exotic birds on a turquoise background. The heavy damask turquoise curtains were drawn across the two floor-to-ceiling bay windows, and another set were hiding the French doors into the garden. No doubt all to keep in the warmth of the fire which flickered in the grate of the elegant, cream-marble surround of the fireplace. It was, however, still a little chilly; Melissa wondered whether she should have dressed more warmly or brought a shawl.

She glanced around, looking for radiators. None seemed to be in evidence. It was odd that some renovations had been done to the house but other, more obvious things, had been left out. On the silver tray, in addition to a selection of spirits, two jugs of cocktails had been prepared – one looked like Pimms, the fruit giving it away, and the other appeared to be Martini; there was a silver server with green olives beside it. There was also a bucket of ice.

Melissa began to pour a couple of Martinis. She hoped they were not too strong otherwise they would be blotto by the end of the evening.

'I met Henry in France, he was a war reporter, damn good one, he also drove ambulances under fire, unarmed – he was very brave,' Alasdair muttered to Melissa, but not so quiet that it obviously couldn't be picked up by the new entrants to the room.

'Brave? That's a bit rich when talking about a conchie,' one of the newcomers spluttered. He was a slim young man with dark features and a small moustache. He spoke with very precise diction. 'Allow me to introduce myself. Godfrey Greenwood. I am a guest of Sir Simon Maundeville. I believe you know him?'

It was Alasdair's turn to splutter. 'Maundeville is here?'

'Standing right beside you, old chap. Give us your hand, long time no see, er, well, you know ...' His voice petered out.

Melissa turned to the pair. 'Delighted to meet you both, I'm sure. Did you also know each other in the war?' She watched as Maundeville and Greenwood exchanged a knowing glance.

'In a manner of speaking.' Maundeville tapped his nose. 'Hush, hush and all that.'

'Ah, spies and underhand dealings – not quite British, is it?' The sharp response came from Henry Blake, who was pouring himself a rather large whisky. Melissa noticed his hand shook.

Greenwood flushed and rounded on Blake; he opened his mouth to speak but was beaten to it by Maundeville. 'Steady, Godfrey, Henry is a distinguished member of the press, don't forget. We must accord him all due courtesy.'

Alasdair frowned. Melissa wondered what he had heard. He seemed to have developed an extraordinary sense of hearing, and picked up nuances in speech that she missed. These had not been missed by Maundeville. He leant close and muttered quietly in Alasdair's ear. 'Still got the nose, I see. I'd like to catch up with you later – after dinner in the library?' He moved on over to the drinks and poured himself a large gin before strolling over to the other side of the room. Greenwood, like a shadow trailing a great man, followed.

There was a piercing high-pitched shriek from the doorway. 'Mellie, darling, you're here. How glorious! You must be the divinely brave Alasdair.' She laid a hand on Alasdair's arm. 'I am Lottie, Mellie's cousin, remember me? Oh!' Another shriek.

Alasdair winced and Melissa smiled. Dear Lottie really had a very high-pitched voice.

'Henry, you are here too. You didn't wait for me.' She turned her huge baby blue eyes upon the man in question and he grinned sheepishly.

'Sorry, Lotts, needed a quick snifter, thought I'd get here first but, er, as it happens, not the case,' he finished rather lamely.

Alasdair grinned. 'We rather had the same thought. Known Lottie long?'

'Yes, don't let her fool you, all those bobbed blonde curls and innocent eyes; she drove an ambulance at the frontline in France for the last year of the war. That's where we met.'

'And you are …?' Alasdair raised one eyebrow.

'Good grief, no, what do I have to offer a gal like her?'

'Don't be silly, Henry.' Lottie pouted. 'You know you are my number one reporter. Anyway' – she lowered her voice in mock conspiracy – 'we are here to inherit, and then who cares who we marry?'

Melissa gave her a long cool look of reproach. 'Even considering benefiting from the deaths of heroic cousins Henry and Richard is just low down. How could you?'

Tears sprang up in Lottie's eyes. 'Oh, Mellie, you know I don't mean it really, it's just – it is so hard with no money.' She rolled her eyes towards her Henry and lowered her voice. 'And with not enough men to go around as well. You were lucky, Mellie, getting in when you did. At least he came back!'

An acerbic comment arose in Melissa; she opened her mouth to speak but was beaten to it when someone caught her arm and swung her around.

'So how is my gorgeous cuz? Still kissing, I hope, sweetie?'

Melissa gave a bright laugh and hugged her cousin George, giving him a chaste peck on the cheek; she noticed Alasdair's top lip curl. 'Only, George, just remember I am still a happily married cuz, have been for some years.' She lightly chastised him, knowing Alasdair would be fuming. George always managed to rub him up the wrong way. 'What about you? Didn't I hear about an engagement pending?'

'S'pose my dear sister has been blabbing, has she? She'll be down shortly. We all came down together – me, Ems and the dreary Rose.' He sighed melodramatically. 'Still, she's loaded, titled, well, an Honourable like you and desperate.' He laughed.

Melissa suddenly remembered all the holidays of torment when she was a child and George was present: frogs in the bed, slugs in the wellies. She shivered; he really could be a reptile. Poor Rose, she thought, and vowed to make it up to her, or better still find her someone nicer than George. She squeezed Alasdair's arm. She was so lucky; he was back and he was wonderful, even if he was a bit of a grump.

At that moment, they were joined by her cousin Emma and another tall athletic-looking young woman. Rose, Melissa presumed. She hadn't seen Emma for over a year and was startled at how wan she looked. She really did not look well, completely strung out as, if she had the world on her shoulders. The fact she was wearing a shapeless black velvet frock did not help. Looking across at Lottie, resplendent in peacock blue which shimmered with sequins and caught the blue flash of her eyes, the contrast in dynamism was dramatic. Really, she must make time to catch up with Emma. Melissa realised that by concentrating on Alasdair over the last few years, she had been woefully remiss about her own family.

'This is the Honourable Rose Tennant. You know, the daughter of Lord Treggwent?' Even Emma's voice was listless. Yes, Melissa thought, they were long overdue a conflab. She shook hands with Rose and winced slightly at the firm handshake. 'How d'you do?'

'Better now.' Rose had a loud, low voice which carried. 'Half term exeat at the mo, thank goodness. No more snotty fourth formers crucifying lacrosse and stabbing themselves with épées.'

Seeing Melissa's startled look, Emma supplied the information necessary to understand this clipped remark. 'Rose teaches. Games at St Bede's, you know?'

Melissa whistled. St Bede's was one of the most prestigious schools in the country, if not the world. One she herself had been quite desperate to attend, but she had failed to convince the baron of the merit of boarding school, so a governess it had been, much to her chagrin. 'Golly, I am impressed. How clever you must be to have a job there.'

'Hardly.' Rose shrugged off the praise. 'And the pupils are little blighters the lot of them.' She bared her teeth in the semblance of a grin, which was momentarily quite terrifying. Melissa hastily amended her view of the school.

There was only enough time for introductions before their hosts joined them. They were accompanied by a good-looking middle-aged man. Melissa recognised him as Arthur Baggeley, who owned the adjoining estate. Beside him was a young man in a dog collar, and she assumed he must be the new local vicar, whom she had heard about through Aunt Honor's regular letters. Really, it was lovely to be back here at Pennstone Manor again. So little had changed; it was all so safe and predictable. She smiled warmly at her aunt and gave her uncle an affectionate peck on the cheek.

'Hello, Brigadier.' Despite being her uncle, he was seldom called anything else. Even Lady Honor called him Brigadier when in public.

He gave a gruff harrumph but coloured in pleasure. He took his wife's arm and whispered as they moved away, 'I can quite see why she's your favourite, me dear.' He glanced back at her handsome husband, and was taken quite aback. 'Good Gad, looking at him you would never know he was blind. Honor, as usual, you are right about everything. It could even turn out just as we've planned.' Giving his wife a quick encouraging smile, he turned his attention to his other guests.

After the introductions were made, the butler hovered,

ready to announce dinner. Melissa wondered why he seemed to be hesitating in the doorway and then all was clear.

'I am so sorry! I appear to be late. Such a faux pas, n'est pas, I am désolé.'

The butler stood back to allow the entrance, and an entrance it was – of a vision in full-length gold lamé. Sir Simon Maundeville almost leapt forward and cried, 'At last, Brigadier Ferguson, Lady Ferguson, may I introduce my surprise guest? The Countess de Orleon.'

THREE

Melissa felt Alasdair tense up beside her. She turned towards him, but he gave an infinitesimal shake of his head. Thus tipped off, she instantly settled to watch, and to remember, in detail, for discussion with Alasdair later; after all, she was now, in effect, his eyes on the world. Any visual detail she might pick up could be vitally important to him. She thought back to that marvellous parlour game, Kim's Game, at which she excelled. Thank goodness for her grandfather, the baron, who had taught her the game so well over many wet afternoons in his study at Castle Brock.

'Sir Simon, thank you so much for arranging the transport for me,' the heavily accented, deep voice almost purred. The Countess stood aside to reveal someone behind her. A small, young, rather mousy-looking woman with the face of a faded Madonna stepped forward rather diffidently. She was dressed simply but elegantly in a grey silk frock. Her hair was in a neat bun. She exuded the charm of a bygone era. 'My companion, Agnés. I absolutely cannot function without her, I hope you do not mind?' The Countess fluttered her eyelashes around the gathering, unsure as yet who was her host.

Melissa spotted Honor signalling to the butler and realised that this was an unexpected addition to the party.

The Countess noticed it too. 'Oh dear, I hope I do not inconvenience you too much, Lady Ferguson. Agnés is very amenable. She can always sleep in the attics …' She flicked her wrist in such a way as to encompass the heights of the house where the servants might sleep. In fact, they had their own end of a wing at the back of the house. 'Have dinner on a tray?' Agnés coloured but kept silent.

'I wouldn't dream of it,' Lady Honor retorted crisply. 'Smithers will have a room prepared while we dine.' She slowly glanced up and down the height of the Countess, taking in the elaborate hairstyle, piled so artfully on her heard, the floor-length gold, haute couture gown, the invasive perfume. 'I see you came dressed in readiness. Such foresight.'

Melissa hid a smile; thus the daughter of a baron put an interloper in her place.

'Beg your pardon, m'lady. I understand we have one further guest?' The butler stood aside to let him through.

'Yes indeed,' Maundeville intoned. 'We also have Colonel Manders with us.'

A good-looking, sandy-haired man in his mid-thirties popped his head round the door frame.

The Countess, who had been leaning on the doorway with dramatic effect, was forced to step aside to let him in. 'Mon dieu, another faux pas. I thought you were the chauffeur.' She let out an affected tinkle of insincere laughter.

It was the turn of Colonel Manders, in full military evening dress, to flush red in the face, and he clearly floundered in finding a suitable response, as, no doubt, the Countess had intended.

Once again, Honor, Lady Ferguson, came to the rescue. 'Colonel, what a pleasure to meet you. It is always a privilege to play hostess to our brave military men.' Then, before anyone could interrupt, she signalled to Smithers, the butler. 'I believe we had better dine before it is ruined and the cook has apoplexy!'

They processed into dinner in a bit of a muddle, with both Maundeville and Colonel Manders attempting to lead the Countess forth. She, however, snubbed both and took the arm of a stunned-looking Greenwood. For a secretary to be plucked from such obscurity could have been a coup. As Melissa looked at him with his pencil moustache, he suddenly reminded her of one of her aunt's schnauzers. If he had been one, he certainly would have been wagging his tail now.

Lady Honor consulted quickly, in hushed tones, with the butler, to no doubt quickly rethink the seating plan. Maundeville also appeared to be adding his own ideas. Melissa hoped he was apologising. At the summons of the – clearly new – electric bell push, staff appeared from behind a concealed door in the oak panel work and added extra places and chairs in a polished routine that was most impressive. During the small pause before they all could be seated, Alasdair muttered to Melissa, 'I thought you said this was going to be a small, select gathering. This is a full-on house party.' He sounded momentarily appalled.

'Honestly, Alasdair,' she replied. 'So did I. I'm as surprised as you, honestly I am.' She squeezed his arm. 'You will be fine, I am here, don't worry.'

'How many are there?' he whispered.

'Let me see ... Brigadier Ferguson, Lady Honor, Arthur Baggeley, the vicar, Lottie, Henry Blake, Emma, George, Rose, Sir Simon Maundeville, Godfrey Greenwood, the Countess, her companion, Colonel Manders, you and me. Gosh, that is fourteen. Good job Agnés was included – thirteen at dinner would have been terrifically unlucky.'

'I could always have dropped out. Saved myself a lot of bother.'

'Don't be silly,' she whispered back. 'It will all be fine.'

Luckily, he could not see the fingers of her other hand crossed behind her back.

FOUR

They were interrupted when the seating had finally been arranged. Melissa only had a few moments to register the glory of the table. Crisp, white linen. The silver, and what silver there was: the cutlery, the two enormous candelabra and the centrepiece. Delightful for her, but traps to ensnare Alasdair? Her stomach gave a little flip of tension. Had she made the most awful mistake in her selfish desire to be here this weekend?

Checking the hastily rearranged seating cards in their silver holders, Melissa found herself sitting between Alasdair and the vicar. She caught Lady Honor's sheepish look and realised that she thought Melissa had been dealt the short straw. However, the vicar's quiet demeanour meant that she was able to concentrate on Alasdair. She was grateful, as she was only too aware that he was as nervous as hell. This would be his first formal dinner, and certainly a lot more public than either of them had intended. She gave a quiet sigh. It had been such a hill to climb to get him here, and she could not bear for it all to go wrong. He might never go out again. She glanced down the table. On the far side of Alasdair was the surprise guest, Agnés, and she seemed to be, at first glance, as reserved as the vicar.

However, with this placement, Melissa realised that Alasdair should be absolutely fine. She had requested that his place be laid with water glasses instead of wine stems, as he did tend to knock these over when stressed. She had already had a discreet word with Smithers, the butler, and all the staff were instructed to treat this foible as if it was absolutely the norm – the mark of all well-trained servants.

Melissa contemplated their own serviced flat in town. It was so much easier in the confines of your own home, but, oh, it was so wonderful to be back at a real dinner party in the company of her family, dressed up in the latest fashions, surrounded with colourful company. The last years had been so hard. Alasdair, so self-conscious and prickly, refusing to accept any invitations or indeed to meet with anyone, even at home. No wonder they thought he was dead.

She turned to Alasdair and proceeded to give him a rundown of the seating arrangements. She had no fears about the cutlery. Alasdair was a stickler for detail. They had practised eating in a formal setting time and time again, until Alasdair was able to reach out his hands and, using his fingertips, gauge the correct knife and fork for each course. There was a small pause while the vicar was called upon to pronounce grace. The first course arrived. It was smoked mackerel pate, served with Melba toast. Melissa began to consider the mechanics of how they were going to handle this. In the end, she just reached over and spread the pate thickly over the toast on his plate. She could almost imagine that his toast was slightly thicker than her own as it did not break and crumble as hers did. She raised her eyes and caught a small nod from Smithers. She nodded back in recognition. Someone had thought this out very carefully; she wondered who they had to thank.

Between courses, they both attempted to engage Agnés and Harold James, the vicar, in conversation but with little success. If anything, Melissa thought, they both seemed in an even worse state of nerves than Alasdair, but then, Alasdair hid his nerves easily. That was why he fooled other people. Thomas, his valet and batman during the war, was the only one who knew the real extent of his weakness. Even with her he was cautious. Was he afraid that she would love him less? Lose respect? Did he fear pity? But that wasn't what she felt. Never.

At least now she had found out the vicar's name. How on earth was he going to cope with his flock if he was this shy? Melissa wondered. He had managed the formal grace at the start of the meal admirably, with only a small quiver in his rather high but clear voice, but that seemed to have exhausted him to such an extent that it had effectively silenced him. It was like pulling teeth. He was going to have to buck up at dinners; if he was overwhelmed here, he was going to have a hard time. The local vicar was the standard preferred extra at all local dinner parties in the country. When numbers were needed, he would be called on, especially a young, apparently single and presumably eligible male.

This lack of active conversation allowed Melissa to sit and observe the dinner party for a few moments. She noticed that the Countess sought to dominate the conversation at every turn and that the men seemed happy to let her. There was much pouting and little moues and enough regular eyelash-fluttering to keep them occupied. She had to restrain a sigh. It was women like the Countess who were setting the Women's Movement back years. Once or twice she caught Honor's eye, and just a slight raising of an eyebrow and a small smile showed Melissa that Lady Honor was finding this just as amusing – or was it bemusing? – as she was.

The next course, fillet of sole, went without mishap, and once finished, Melissa found her thoughts wandering. What were all these people doing here? Why now? She looked across the table. Opposite them was her cousin Emma, almost concealed by an enormous silver epergne filled with autumn fruits and trailing greenery. Emma, what could see of her, really did not look well. She was pale, fidgeting, and appeared to be making no effort, with Colonel Manders one side and Arthur Baggeley on the other. She should have been in seventh heaven: a good-looking man without encumbrance on either side of her. There really was such a paucity of men since the war; it was hard to meet new ones, and they were snapped up with often unseemly haste by the marriage market. She should not be sitting there twisting her hanky – or was it her napkin? – in her lap. What a drip Emma was being. It all added to the frisson of uneasiness that had crept over Melissa, emphasising a growing feeling that this weekend was somehow unusual. She just hoped they would learn more after dinner. It all really was most perplexing. What was going on?

Wonderfully moist roast chicken breast and vegetables were served next, finally followed by raspberry charlotte russes with fresh cream. They must have access to a glasshouse, thought Melissa wistfully. It was late in the season for fresh raspberries. Still, they had survived, and she squeezed Alasdair's thigh under the table to congratulate him.

Of course, after dinner all the men stayed on, as was customary, for the port and cigars, with the exception of Colonel Manders, who muttered about work. Brigadier Ferguson seemed to be determined to keep up appearances from before the war.

The ladies were expected to repair to the second drawing room. A custom, perhaps not so much kept now in town, but in the country the old customs still held. Melissa hated leaving Alasdair but knew better than to make a fuss. He would have to fend for himself for a short while.

The Countess, however, had no such sensitivities. She gave a moue of displeasure at being separated from the men and all but flounced out. Lottie, coming up behind, nudged Melissa and grinned. Melissa grinned back; this promised to be some fun, she thought, as they followed the Countess's petulant hip sashay down the hall rather more sedately.

Meanwhile, in the dining room the men were passing the port and some were puffing away on the high-quality Havana cigars being proffered by the Brigadier. Alasdair sat quietly, not partaking of the port or the cigars, nervous that he might knock over the glass. He found that cigars affected his sense of smell, so important a sense to him now. It was bad enough that the smell of the candles burning on the table distracted him. He was nervous of making any large gestures. What if he knocked over one of the candelabra? The heat still coming from them was phenomenal. He checked himself, told himself to calm down; he needed to be in the present, not worrying about what might happen. That way lay madness and accidents.

Having noticed his abstinence, Maundeville leant across and said, 'Shall we tootle off to have our little chat? I thought the library would suit?' He stood up and then realised that some accommodation was necessary to get Alasdair from the room and into the library.

After they left, back in the dining room, George could not resist commenting. 'Poor old Alasdair. Must be really hard for him, having been such a man of action.' Insincerity dribbled from his lips. 'Being forced to hang onto another man's arm, looking like he bats for the other team, must be galling.' A stunned silence greeted his comment.

'Well really, George, even though you are my nephew, you sometimes take the biscuit,' exploded the Brigadier.

'Now, Uncle, you know how these things can get out of hand, how any little slur of that nature could ruin a man's career, don't you know?'

'Well, that is the last thing anyone would think of Alasdair. Enough said, man.'

George looked slyly around the table, noting the facial expressions. Two birds with one stone, he thought. The Brigadier might bluster, but there was surely no way he would make the wife of a blind man his heir. Perhaps a little reinforcement was needed.

'Anyone for shooting tomorrow?' He turned to Greenwood. 'You a good shot?'

Greenwood looked taken aback. 'Well, I can shoot, but I believe Sir Simon will have me working much of the weekend.'

'What about you, Vicar?' George now attempted a snipe at another victim.

'Oh dear me no, not quite within my calling, I prefer the quieter pursuits.'

'Wife-hunting yet? I'd have thought having a little woman at your side was essential out here in the sticks.'

The vicar flushed. 'Oh, not quite ready for that, new here, need to settle in.'

'Absolutely, no need to rush into anything,' Arthur Baggeley stated genially. He was a kind man and clearly had enough of this baiting. 'George, Brigadier Ferguson has an excellent estate manager, fine fellow. I'll pop over and have a word with him before breakfast. He'll sort something out for you, might put up some pheasant in the woods. If so, I might be tempted to join you.'

FIVE

I n the library, Maundeville had led Alasdair to one of
the two high-backed leather wing chairs in front of the
fire. Alasdair sank into it with a sigh. A safe haven at
last. It was so daunting putting your trust in someone else
– exhausting, in fact. He sat recovering, gripping the arms
of the chair tightly until his heartbeat returned to normal.

Maundeville threw a couple of logs on the fire, and
it crackled with surprising venom in response. 'So, down
to business. We have a problem. In our network there is a
rogue agent. Been there some time, I have no doubt. The
thought that they might have been there during the war is
stinking. Positively bloody. Literally. It is just possible they
may have been responsible for your own little show.'

'You think so?' Alasdair frowned; he would dearly like
to know who it was that had whacked him in the dark hard
enough to detach his retinas. For a moment, he could smell
the smoke of the ruins of the bombed-out church. Some
of the pews had been still hot to the touch. He could hear
the crump of the guns in the near distance. The crump that
masked the footsteps of the person he had been tracking.
Then blackness, darkness and nightmares.

'Yes, that is where you come in. You were my best agent. Now that you've lost your sight, it doesn't change that. In fact, we can use it to our significant advantage. Consider yourself seconded back on the team. You are a canny lad, wouldn't have made major so quick in the war otherwise. Listen, sit in the shadows, form your conclusions. I bet most people think you've lost your wits as well as your sight, and most importantly, only tell me what you find out. No one else.' He paused and then added, as if on an afterthought. 'Oh, and you can include your wife. You could make a good team!'

'I will not put her in any danger.' Alasdair's glance in Sir Simon's direction was fierce.

'Do you know, Alasdair, I could swear you can see me. Why, you even appear to make eye contact.'

'Practice, and I have had sight, don't forget. It's simple. I can hear where a mouth is and look up a touch. Now don't divert me. We were talking about Melissa.'

'You don't give her enough credit. She grew up in the countryside, crack shot, excellent horsewoman, fit, and above all, intelligent to boot!'

'Done your homework, I see. This wasn't a casual meeting, was it? I'm not denying what you are saying but it's just … Oh, I give her credit, but give her an inch …'

'Yes, yes, but she must be bored stupid …' Maundeville's voice tapered off.

'Looking after a blind man,' Alasdair completed, trying for bravado but not quite making it.

'No, man, damn it, I mean having been stuck in that flat all this time. Weren't you climbing the walls?'

'Only when I could find them,' came Alasdair's dry

response. He always hid his pain in humour; even Melissa was not witness to his darkest moments. It was bad enough she was reduced to leading him around like a useless lump without her being privy to his innermost thoughts and emotions. He could not let go, relax his guard. If he sank into the mire, what would he find? Bones, flesh, rats as in the trenches, all pervaded by the sense of fear? He straightened his shoulders. 'So, tell me more. What are we looking for?'

Half an hour later, after discussing his thoughts and suspicions, all too thin for Alasdair's liking, Maundeville made his excuses and left.

What the hell do I do now? thought Alasdair. The bugger has only gone and left me. I'm stuck here like a fly in butter. Time passed. He opened his Braille watch and felt for the hands with his fingertips – ten o'clock, still early. Eventually Melissa would notice him missing and come looking for him. God, he was lucky. As an aristocrat, she could have had anybody and yet she chose him, and look how that had turned out – saddled with a blind man.

The fire was warm and he began to doze, then he heard the door open behind him. He was about to call out when he realised the whispered conversation was not meant for his ears, and it was apparent that the people could not see him. Was he sitting in the shadows? Had Maundeville turned off the lights? He silently slid lower in the chair and lifted up his feet. It was a shame Maundeville had thrown on those logs; the crackle of the fire as they went up was making it hard to eavesdrop. It appeared to be a man and a woman, the tone of the conversation furtive and antagonistic. He could not make out anything that the woman was saying. Her tone was conciliatory and terrified in turns.

The man's voice, a low rasp, could only be made out when he lost his patience. Alasdair heard, 'Hold your nerve! Don't do anything stupid.'

Then, in a louder, aggressive hiss. 'If you do anything that lets me down, you're dead. I'll not face the consequences.' The door closed with a sharp click.

Alasdair waited. He could just detect heavy breathing. Maybe sobbing? Then the door opened and clicked shut again. He grimaced. If only Melissa would come along now, maybe she would see who it was.

Time, however, continued to pass. Another twenty minutes. Alasdair, steepling his fingers, rested his chin on them. The rarefied silence of the library, the smell of the leather books and the crackle of the fire accompanied his reflections on the hushed conversation he had just, barely, heard. The voices were so low and stressed that he couldn't put a name to them. Voices change with emotion, altering the cadences, making them harder to identify.

The door burst open. 'Alasdair, Alasdair, are you there?' Melissa sounded frantic.

'Yes, I am here. It's been an interesting hour.'

'You have no idea. I have so much to tell you. The Countess probably eats small children for breakfast – raw. Emma is behaving very oddly, and Lottie is acting as though she is about to explode. Then, finally, the men joined us, and you were missing, so I thought maybe they had abandoned you in the dining room. That was empty, and then I remembered Maundeville and the library. Anyway, we must be quick – the Brigadier has an announcement to make.'

SIX

They progressed to the main green drawing room at quite a pace. Alasdair could feel Melissa's excitement and tension through her arm as the muscles under his fingers tensed and relaxed and her arm gave the occasional involuntary twitch. Something had wound her up.

'Slow down a moment,' he almost shouted. 'You'll have me bouncing off the walls in a minute.'

'Sorry, darling, but I just don't want to miss anything. There really is something going on.'

But before they could make their way to the room, a terrific commotion took place at the front door as they stood poised in the entrance hall. A loud hammering and shouting could be heard, and the parlour maid rushed to open it. Melissa looked around for the butler, the person she expected to be answering that door, just as he appeared at the drawing room threshold. He had clearly been attending to the needs of the occupants in there.

A tall, corpulent barrel of a man stood dripping on the entrance steps, outrage pouring off him as well as the water, for those aware enough to see it. His features were dark under a large-brimmed felt hat.

'Good Gad! I have nearly been run off the road this evening. Car's virtually in a ditch. What sort of idiots do you allow to drive down here? Brigadier, where are you, man? I've had to walk miles. Why didn't you send out a search party?'

The butler walked over swiftly, divested the man of his coat and hat in one smooth motion and said, 'You must be Bernard Lyon? Your office telephoned to say that you would be delayed. We were not expecting you until tomorrow, sir.'

'What utter rot! Who called?'

'Well, well, Bernard, at least you are here now,' interrupted the bluff tones of the Brigadier. 'You look completely soaked and thoroughly done in. Have you eaten?' In reply to a terse shake of the head, he continued, 'Look, we'll get the housekeeper to draw you a hot bath and I am sure cook can rustle up something on a tray in your room. Smithers, get the man a brandy, he looks like he needs it. I've just got some family business to conclude here and then I'll come up for a chat. How's that?'

The man did indeed look done in, and he sank onto a large ornately carved wooden hall chair. Melissa cast her eyes about the hall, memorising the scene to describe it to Alasdair later. He would probably want to pace it out. He spent most of his time counting his footsteps to improve his spatial awareness. There were several of these chairs dotted about the large, almost gothic entrance hall. In the middle was a round table with matching ornately carved legs. On it stood a huge floral arrangement in a blue and white Wedgwood vase. In a corner was a suit of armour – heaven only knows how long that had been there. Meanwhile, the stranger quietly dripped, his trouser bottoms and his muddy shoes marking the beautiful rug by the fire.

Melissa, who had daringly taken on the occasional bit of housework in their flat to minimise disruption to Alasdair, grimaced ruefully as she thought of the work that would be involved to remove the marks. Perhaps, after this weekend, she could persuade Alasdair to go out and then the flat could be serviced properly. That was, after all, what they paid for.

The Brigadier waved his hands at the family and ushered them back into the living room, much like a shepherd and his sheep. Melissa and Alasdair tagged on behind and walked into the blue drawing room; a maid slipped in as well, no doubt to serve more alcoholic drinks and coffee. She discreetly motioned to Melissa that there were two dining chairs against the far wall. There was a grand piano centre stage in the bay window; Melissa also spied, with some delight, a modern-looking gramophone. She speculated that some frivolity could be in the offing for the weekend. There were enough of the young things to get up some dance partners. She just hoped that there would not be some tedious piano recitals for the oldies. Perhaps somewhere there might be some jazz records. She prayed that the men would not spend all their time either shooting or playing billiards and grimaced as she realised that these were two occupations Alasdair would not partake of, even if he wanted to. She wondered what his feelings were, if he had thought it through. Was this behind his reticence to come on these weekends? They had been invited enough times over the years. Did he think that his inability to indulge in these masculine pursuits made him less of a man? Would they ever be able to talk about this together out in the open? Alasdair was not really a feelings man, and she had a sneaking suspicion that he never would be, but somehow they had to find a way to move on.

Melissa picked her way across the room with Alasdair ably walking with her. When they got to the chairs, she guided his hand to the chair back and said, 'Good old Smithers. He's kept two chairs for us.'

Brigadier Ferguson stood up and cleared his throat rather self-consciously. 'Look, I am going to have to keep this short. Bernard will kick up a stink otherwise.'

'Who is he, Uncle?' Lottie looked bewildered.

'Oh, Lotts, you are so out of touch,' George drawled. 'That, my dear, was the eminent merchant banker, Bernard Lyon. Made the bank a fortune during the war, a great war effort,' he sneered.

'You know, for once I agree with your cousin,' Alasdair muttered sotto voce to Melissa.

'That's as may be.' There was nothing wrong with the Brigadier's hearing. 'He is my guest this weekend and he will be treated as such.' There was a touch of steel in his voice that brooked no argument. He took a deep breath and then plunged on, his voice softening. 'Now to our family business. As you know, I have invited down this weekend all the remaining family cousins …' He cleared his throat. '… from both my family and from Honor's. We have decided that the time has come for us to settle our affairs. Neither of us are getting any younger, don't you know? And with the boys gone …' He cleared his throat again.

'Well, we thought it would be a good idea for you to come down here and see the lie of the land, decide if the country life could suit you. To see if Honor and I think you have it in you to take over Pennstone Manor and continue our legacy. I shall be having my solicitor down on Monday to draw up a new will. That is why Bernard is here to advise me.'

Was it Melissa's imagination or had a collective gasp gone around the room?

'No, don't get into a panic, your original legacies will all be safe, but I need to look to the future of the estate.'

'Oh, here, here, Uncle,' George exclaimed. 'What a brave and excellent decision. Look to the future, what? What?'

Melissa choked back a giggle as she saw Lottie miming being sick behind George's back. This statement of her uncle's came as no real surprise, especially as Lottie herself had raised it earlier. She wondered fleetingly if this would mean that Lottie could now get married, if she inherited the estate and if Henry Blake would have her. She somehow could not think they would want to move to the country. The Honourable Charlotte Dauncey, to be completely accurate, was the epitome of the 'Bright Young Thing' so salaciously written up in the tabloid press. Still, perhaps it had palled; they both seemed to carry the war heavily on their shoulders.

'Bit dangerous that, don't you think?' Alasdair whispered in her ear.

'What do you mean?'

'Well, if someone is really determined to inherit the pile, then they might try to reduce the odds.'

'With George that is a foregone conclusion – he is a total ass.'

'Does that mean he might not resort to murder if push came to shove?'

Melissa shrugged, then remembering, added, 'I am not sure.'

'Ah, but how far do you think he might go?'

Melissa spluttered, 'Be serious, Alasdair. This is Cousin George we are talking about. Get a grip. He wasn't even fit enough to fight in the war!'

Coffee came, served in tiny bone china demitasse cups of startling emerald green and with gold interiors. The other guests then joined them, wandering in from the green drawing room, bringing a livelier atmosphere to the rather stunned family group. Liqueurs were drunk from crystal glasses. The gramophone remained silent; no one seemed inclined to search around for some suitable music. The time moved on. Conversation now ebbed and flowed in a desultory manner. However, under it all, Melissa sensed a frisson of excited tension. It had been a very strange evening. Alasdair yawned. Melissa realised that this must have been exhausting for him, especially on top of the train journey down here, and so suggested that they retired early.

The room had begun to fug up rather uncomfortably with cigarette smoke. Most of her family, the young ones at least, and the Countess, seemed to smoke endlessly. So they said their goodnights and went on up. They had been lucky in that they had been accorded one of the double rooms in the family wing; she just hated twin beds. There were two wings to the house of some twelve bedrooms. She wondered how many bathrooms there were now and which bedrooms had been sacrificed to accommodate them. Their room was large and comfortable with a bay window, in which there was a seating area and even a small writing desk. The rest of the furniture was large, mahogany and Victorian: a huge wardrobe, dressing table and tall chest of drawers, upon which was a glass-covered, revolting, stuffed bird scene. The fire had thankfully been lit and threw a romantic glow into the room. There was plenty of light for her to see by. There appeared to be no electric light in this room and rather than light the oil lamp, she moved it away from the bedside table and put it on the chest of drawers so it helped obscure the birds, whose glass eyes seemed to catch the firelight, making them appear alive once more. Using the firelight to undress by, Melissa was pleasantly surprised to discover that Alasdair was not that tired after all. Later, they collapsed into a satisfied slumber.

***

With an almighty crash, the body hit the antiquated suit of armour that had been quietly rusting in the corner of the grand entrance hall. It responded by collapsing across the body, masking the method of murder. At four o'clock in the morning, there were still embers in the grate of the great hall fireplace, a sculpted sandstone monstrosity, but they lent a cosy light to the gruesome scene. It was the kind of crash that caused innocent sleepers to awake with a start, to jump out of bed and appear, tousle-haired and wide-eyed, from both wings of the house, in the upstairs corridors, outside their bedrooms. It also was the kind of crash that allowed the murderer to slip away unnoticed in the confusion and reappear with the rest of the household as if awoken afresh from an innocent sleep, surprised.

Melissa awoke with a start and leapt out of bed in shock. They tumbled out onto the landing, Alasdair clinging onto Melissa's arm. 'What the hell?' he began.

'Everyone, stay still,' Sir Simon Maundeville's voice commanded. 'Brigadier, are you there? Good, let us go down and investigate first.'

But they were too late – a high-pitched scream and then a wailing that went on and on came up from the floor below.

'All right, everyone,' the Brigadier Ferguson shouted up. 'Go back to your rooms and stay there.' He sounded breathless. 'There has been an accident. Sir Simon is telephoning colleagues in London. We will talk to you as soon as we can.'

'What's happening?' Alasdair hissed to Melissa. 'No, no don't go down – look over the banisters,' he instructed when he realised she might leap impetuously down the stairs and investigate.

'Good grief,' she exclaimed. 'You were right about dangerous times. Oh, I just knew there was something wrong this evening. I had such a bad feeling as it progressed.' She began to cry. 'Alasdair, darling, what a horror. There is a body down there, covered in the fallen armour. On the hall rug.'

SEVEN

'Quick, stand back. Take us back to the room.' Once inside, Alasdair said, 'Lock the door. No, don't interrupt. Tell me everything you saw.'

'Oh, Alasdair. Alasdair, it was horrible.' Melissa's voice rose, bordering on hysteria.

'Keep calm, breathe, tell me all. Now.' The command in his voice quietened her rising hysterics.

'Well, there was a body on the floor near the fireplace in the hall. Looked like the old suit of armour had fallen over it.'

Keeping his voice low and steady, Alasdair encouraged her. 'Go on, my darling, everything as you saw it. I know it is awful, but we need to understand what is going on.'

'Well, it was a woman, well, I assume so – pink dressing gown, slim legs. Oh, so undignified. Who can it be? The armour obscured the top half of the body. She had sensible slippers.' She began hyperventilating.

'Stay calm. Breathe slowly. This is not the time for an attack of the vapours'.

Melissa's head snapped up and she glared at him; he felt it and grinned. He knew she would rally with enough provocation.

'There is no point in speculating,' he said. 'I was afraid of something like this. The whole place is a tinderbox. What is Brigadier Ferguson thinking?'

'That really is unfair!'

'No. It isn't. I could smell this sort of thing during the war. I could always tell when the tensions between the men in a trench were about to blow. Unless, of course, the Brigadier Ferguson is being used. Maundeville isn't here for fun, that's for a start. I wonder what—'

The handle on the door turned and then there was a discreet tap. Alasdair nodded at Melissa. She smiled, a rush of love releasing some of the tension. 'Sometimes I could swear you can see me,' she muttered as she opened the door. The man in question, Maundeville, stood there.

'So, the hares are running. The game begins. Ready for action, Alasdair? Good. Melissa, what about you? Alasdair, fill her in, then she can escort you down to the library. I have commandeered it as an office.' He turned and was gone.

'What? A game?'

'Jolly good, Mellie. I'll explain, meant to last night but, to be frank, I was exhausted.'

'You could have fooled me. Tired in mind, was it?'

'Very amusing, didn't you…?'

'Oh shut up and spill the beans!'

'Sir Simon wasn't so far off when he was talking about a game. It is the greatest game. The King's Game.'

Melissa's raised her eyebrows, momentarily startled into not giving an audible reply for a few moments. 'You mean you were a spy?' she managed eventually.

'Something like that. As you know, I always had an ear for languages.'

'Yes, French governesses and relations in Austria.' Melissa's voice grew waspish.

'Distant relations in Austria. Still, all those summers hiking in the Tyrol paid off. I can speak German fluently and brushed up my French to almost pass as a native.'

'Did you now? And just how did you do that?' Melissa crossed her arms in front of her chest.

Alasdair was unable to see it but heard the tone in her voice. 'Look, stop distracting me or we will be here all night. This is a bad situation made worse. Maundeville had no idea I was going to be here. Well, I think that is the case. Maybe he did, but anyway. He is here on business, has some idea about unmasking a war spy for the other side. Asked me to help and to recruit you. I had no idea that something like this would happen. Although the signs were there. How could I have missed them? Damn this blindness. This all takes me back to the war.' A slight shiver ran through him.

Suddenly frightened, Melissa jumped in. 'But it might be an accident, surely.'

Alasdair looked her way, exasperation written on his face. 'Quick then, let us get dressed, and then lead on, Macduff, is it? And we can find out.'

'No,' Melissa wailed. 'Not the Scottish Play.'

A very short time later, Melissa, with Alasdair firmly gripping her arm, presented herself at the main library. Someone had thrown another couple of logs on the fire to take the chill off the room. A coffee jug and cups were on a tray on the library table. Sir Simon sat at the only desk in the room, commandeered so that it dominated a cleared space with a couple of dining chairs in front of it. Godfrey Greenwood hovered at his elbow. On seeing Melissa and

Alasdair, Sir Simon waved him away. 'Leave us a moment, Greenwood, shouldn't take long. These two are harmless. Yes, go, shut the door behind you.'

'I say—' began Melissa, but she was silenced by another imperious hand gesture from Maundeville.

'Look,' he hissed quietly, 'this is going to be hard for you two, but the premise of it is brilliant. No one will suspect you. They are far more likely to be open and indiscreet, thinking Alasdair is retarded and you a fluffy aristo.'

'Now, look here.'

'Keep your voice down, girl, I am trying to protect you, and I need you. If you are not up for it then this is the time to say.'

Melissa glanced at Alasdair. His colour was up, his eyes sparkled and one could feel the excitement coming from him. It was easy to tell he wanted this chance. Melissa hadn't seen him so upbeat since he had been blinded. Maybe this was just what he needed to seal his route to recovery. 'No, we are in. What do you want me to do? And who on earth is dead?'

'Oh, Lord. Look, leave Alasdair here in one of those wing chairs.' They moved to the chair. 'That will be perfect. Now, Melissa, I am sorry to say that the dead woman is Emma Ferguson. She has been stabbed. Murdered.'

'Oh.' Melissa's hand went to her mouth, her eyes wide with shock.

'Good Gad, man, she is her cousin, have a care.' Melissa had sat abruptly on the other wing chair and Alasdair reached out for her hand, unerring – he could always pinpoint her exact presence.

'Look,' Maundeville continued in a softer tone, 'I

haven't got time for sentimentality. I need to know if this is connected to my show or if it is just coincidence. Scotland Yard, in fact Special Branch, has given me two days, and then they will send one of their men to take over.'

'But how can it be?' Melissa frowned. 'Emma can't possibly be a spy. That is absurd.'

'But is it, Mellie? Haven't you noticed how many people here have an active connection to the war or France?'

'Yes, but you said yourself Brigadier Ferguson was playing with fire, announcing to us all he was looking for an heir to the estate last night.'

'Did he, by jove? That might put quite a different complexion on it, you are right. The problem is, we just don't know now. The waters are too muddied. What I want you to do, Melissa, is to go up to your family, break the news, watch, listen and learn.'

Melissa looked from one man to the other. 'You are asking me to spy for you on my own family?' Her voice came out as a squeak.

'Yes, I am, if it is relevant to this crime, and a crime it is. Most likely committed by someone in this house. Don't forget – there are others here too. Others we suspect of betraying this country.'

Melissa's body relaxed. 'Of course, you are right. It can't be the family at all. What was I thinking?'

EIGHT

SATURDAY MORNING

What was I thinking indeed? Melissa considered an hour later, as she tried to recollect events ready to report to Alasdair and Maundeville. She yawned. Lord, she was tired. Lack of sleep and the heavy, dark suspicions that refused to stop circling. It was as if Maundeville had opened a Pandora's box in relation to her family. Something dark had escaped and there would be no going back. She made her way wearily down the stairs and slumped in a chair in the hall. She was intensely grateful that the body of her cousin had been removed. To where? The armour had hastily been rearranged but seemed precariously close to collapsing again.

She first made her way to the suite of rooms that her aunt and uncle occupied. Lady Honor was there and appeared to be in the middle of attempting to calm the hysterics of a young parlour maid. 'That will be all, Meg. Now remember what I said.' The maid bobbed a curtsey and nearly ran from the room.

'And what did you say?' Melissa enquired.

'Oh dear, she had some cock and bull story of hearing a

noise and being downstairs in the kitchen when the ruckus started, and now she is convinced she is about to be arrested and hung for murder. I ask you, the stupidity of servants never ceases to amaze me.'

Melissa raised an eyebrow; she had forgotten how old her Aunt Honor was – really positively Victorian. It was hardly the parlour maid's fault she had never been educated.

'What had she seen or heard?' she settled for asking. No point trying to change entrenched ideas at this juncture.

'Nothing I can fathom, but someone will have to question her when she has calmed down.'

I should be making a note of this, thought Melissa, before I forget it. The 'fluffy-headed aristo' comment still irked.

Lady Honor smiled, opened a drawer in her dressing table and extracted a leather-bound notebook with a silver propelling pencil attached. She handed it over. 'Will this be useful? I have about twenty of the things.' In response to Melissa's raised eyebrows, she added, 'Thank-you presents on the whole.'

'This is wonderful, Aunt Honor, how thoughtful of you. You must be a mind-reader.' She may be old-fashioned but there are no flies on Aunt Honor crossed Melissa's mind before she continued, carefully, 'Sir Simon has asked Alasdair and I to be sort of liaison with the family.'

'Well, Alasdair won't be much use, so I guess it will fall all on you. You are sure it's not too much? Bit of a cheek, really. Still, Brigadier Ferguson will want to interfere, I'm sure.'

Melissa bit the inside of her cheek to stop the automatic riposte that rose to refute Lady Honor's assumptions. Servant prejudice she could let go, but when it was Alasdair ... She realised with sharp insight that this, spread before her now, was the future prejudice she would have to deal with. In her rush to shove Alasdair out into the world, she had awoken the innate British aversion to 'other'. She had read about other disabled soldiers being ignored and forgotten but had never thought of the consequences for her own life. Would blind always equal stupid? She rushed into speech, worried she had been silent for too long. 'Well, Sir Simon is being kind to Alasdair. They were in the war together, you know.'

'Really? Yes, such a tragedy, dear, I gather he was highly decorated. What a glittering career he could have had.'

Melissa was now sinking her nails into her palms with suppressed fury. Completely oblivious, Lady Honor continued, unconsciously echoing Maundeville. 'Now, to business. What needs doing?'

Melissa realised with a jolt that Lady Honor appeared to know nothing. She had not herself planned to be the bearer of bad news. 'Well, I clearly need to inform you that Emma is dead.' She rather blurted it out in her rush to get it over with.

'Dead?' echoed Lady Honor. 'Dead.' She went very pale. Worried, Melissa turned and started for the bell pull. Upstairs was still on the old wire system. 'No, no, just give me a glass of water. There is some on my nightstand.' Melissa took the glass, which was positioned as a lid, and poured water from the crystal water decanter. Her aunt took a few sips and her colour returned. 'How on earth are we going to tell her parents?' Ever practical.

'At least it will be something for Uncle Reggie, Brigadier Ferguson, to do,' Melissa replied lamely.

'What about George? The poor boy.' Lady Honor covered her mouth with her hand. Melissa noted with concern that it trembled. 'Reggie said there had been an accident and I assumed it was that dreadful Frenchie.'

'Mmm,' mused Melissa. 'Why?'

'Well, she is rather awful, isn't she? And she seems like the sort of person that things happen to, don't you think?'

'Or perhaps happen around her. Still, I had better see if George is all right. What time is it?' Melissa glanced at her watch – five thirty, where had the time gone? Giving her aunt a kiss on the cheek, she left and made her way to George's room.

She gave a gentle knock and then opened the door, expecting George to be up and about; instead, he was fast asleep and snoring, his dark hair curly and tousled and his face boyish and young, relaxed in sleep.

Melissa stood there in the doorway, unsure what to do. He was her cousin, but then he was a single man. Was this appropriate? Well, murder was hardly appropriate, and it was his sister. However, all decisions were taken from her when the Brigadier fairly bellowed, as was his way, behind her. 'Good Gad! The boy's gone back to bed. Doesn't he know what's happened?'

Melissa shook her head and grimaced, putting her hand up to stem the anticipated flow.

'George, boy, wake up, you idiot. How can he sleep at a time like this? Emma's dead.'

'Dead? Emma?' George started awake and sat up abruptly. 'Don't be daft. Is this a joke?' Then he must have registered the look on the Brigadier's face. 'She really is dead?' His mouth fell open, tears dropped to his cheeks and he began to make raw heaving breaths ending in a sob as he threw himself round and attempted to get out of bed.

Melissa rushed over and sat on the bed beside him. She laid a hand on his shoulder.

'Now, pull yourself together, man, get dressed and assemble downstairs for breakfast pronto,' barked Sir Reginald, before executing a perfect drill turn and leaving the room.

Melissa noticed that he had left the door ajar, she assumed for propriety. 'Oh, George, I don't know what to say. I am so sorry.' He had half risen but sank back to sit on the edge of the bed beside her.

'It's such a shock, and a damned nuisance. We had plans.' He stopped short and rubbed his eyes, turning away from her. 'What happened? Some sort of accident?'

'No, she was murdered, George. What can be going on?'

'Murdered, but she is the only one who …' Again, he stopped, and this time was not quick enough to conceal the sly, almost calculating look that flitted across his features before turning his head away again.

Any sympathy Melissa may have felt for George also flitted away. 'If you know something, then you must tell Maundeville. He has until Monday to investigate before Scotland Yard arrives.'

'Yes, yes.' George waved an irritated hand at her, his mind clearly occupied, and, she felt, not with grief for his sister any more.

Melissa stood up. 'Well, I must let you get dressed. Try

and see if you can eat some breakfast. It is liable to be a long day – the house is in uproar.'

'I bet it is,' George muttered. 'And it is going to get worse.'

NINE

Meanwhile, in the study, Alasdair had been sitting, as instructed, in the wing chair. Facing the fire, his back to the room, he had sat and listened.

Godfrey Greenwood was first in and clearly felt he was above investigation. Alasdair smiled as he listened to Sir Simon. 'So, just to eliminate you, Godfrey, as I need your help as my secretary – you know you are vital. Perhaps you could run though what happened after dinner last night?'

'What, really? You would question me?' Alasdair could hear the outrage tinged with something else. Was it fear?

'Just to eliminate you first,' Maundeville repeated mildly. Greenwood huffed, was silent for a few moments then clearly acquiesced through some visual signal that Alasdair missed. 'Anything interesting happen over the port after we left?'

'We … Oh, what is he doing here? This is outrageous! He is not part of our investigation, surely …'

'Now, now, Alasdair is just here enjoying the fire. He's out of the way, just ignore him. I'm sure he is not interested in what you might have to say. Leave him be – unfair to disturb him, don't you know?'

It was as much as Alasdair could do not to snort with laughter. Would people really accept that his blindness put him in his dotage?

'So,' Sir Simon prompted. 'Over the port?'

'Well, other than that George character being quite obnoxious.' There was real loathing in his voice. 'Now, if he had been murdered, I might have understood it.'

'Really? What was the problem?'

There was a shuffle of movement then Godfrey said, 'He is just a nasty bully and clearly smarming up to Brigadier Ferguson at all costs.'

'Anything else?'

'Well, it is clear that Brigadier Ferguson has the family down for some big powwow. They are all highly strung about something, definitely.'

'And after port?'

'The family were all called to some private meeting, so I grabbed another coffee and went up to my room to do some work before bed.'

'What, not down here?'

'I wanted to escape the atmosphere. The family were clearly agitated and I wanted none of it.' Godfrey's voice had risen.

'You stayed in your room the rest of the evening?'

'Visited the bathroom a couple of times.'

'See anyone else?'

'No, all was quiet, must have switched the light off about half past eleven, next thing I knew there was all the screaming.'

'And, when you came out of your room, who did you see?' Maundeville kept up the pressure.

'Not sure.'

Alasdair sensed a genuine hesitation; he was picking his words with care.

'I am on the wing with the less immediate family, and it was confusing. Let me see ... I think that I saw the conchie, and the French female companion. Oh, and the girl who came down with that George creature, and you, of course ...'

'So you didn't see the Countess then?'

'No.'

'At any time?'

Why is he labouring this? thought Alasdair.

'No, I assumed she was a sound sleeper,' Greenwood commented drily.

'Very well, that will be all. Shall we adjourn for breakfast?'

Alasdair flipped up his watch and felt the Braille; it was indeed seven o'clock. Breakfast started early in the country. His stomach rumbled as if in response to the time. Once Greenwood had exited the room, he asked, 'What are your thoughts?'

'Two, really. As she is family, that is most likely to be the root of it, but I would also dearly like more information on the so-called Countess.'

'Ah, so that is where your suspicions lie?'

'Highly probable,' Sir Simon said. 'I can use this investigation to pep up my own enquiries. If it wasn't for the death itself, this turn of events would have been a godsend.'

I am not sure Melissa would agree, thought Alasdair; he had rather assumed his wife was fond of her quiet cousin. He had sensed a vulnerability about Emma, even though they had only exchanged a few words in all the time he had known her. She had always been the quiet cousin. He had found increasingly, since he had lost his sight, that he had gained a sense of atmosphere, an uncanny knack of putting his finger on the pulse of a situation that many others missed. Perhaps they were distracted by all that they could see and failed to tune into the emotional resonances about them.

A gong sounded and there was a quiet knock at the door. Melissa entered the room to accompany Alasdair to breakfast. She seemed very distracted and even bumped him into the door frame, which was quite unlike her usual carefulness. He often felt that Melissa thought he was made of eggshells. However, they were soon across the hall and into the dining room, and any opportunity for confidential conversation was lost. The dining room was set for breakfast. Alasdair was overwhelmed with the glorious smell of a traditional full English breakfast. He just hoped it was good. His stomach rumbled loudly again.

Breakfast was a standard self-service affair, with huge covered silver dishes arranged on the sideboard, toast and heated jugs of coffee, hot milk and an incongruous brownstone teapot with hand-knitted cosy.

Seeing Melissa's amused glance, Lady Honor, who was seated at the head of the table, commented, 'Thought we should all muck in as best we can this morning, leave the staff free. I understand a constable is questioning them below.'

'A constable? I thought Sir Simon Maundeville was handling this?'

'Well, yes, but we hardly need concern ourselves with servants – the constable will alert us if need be.'

Alasdair grimaced – a mistake, he thought – and resolved to get Melissa and himself questioning them as soon as possible.

Melissa, her equilibrium evidently restored for the moment, deftly steered Alasdair to one of two free chairs in the centre of one side of the table with their backs to the light. Even though he was considered blind, Alasdair still seemed to have a sensitivity to light; whenever possible, he preferred his back to it. His stomach rumbled again in anticipation as he detected the distinctive smell of bacon, fried eggs and was that black pudding?

Some twenty minutes later, having stuffed himself with a breakfast supplied by his wonderful wife, no servants being in attendance, he turned to her. 'Shall we go for a walk? After this breakfast, I will need it to keep me awake—'

'Good idea,' Brigadier Ferguson interrupted. 'I'll join you and introduce Davies, my new estate manager. I think you might find him interesting.'

Not sure I will, thought Alasdair, annoyed. He had been looking forward to some time alone with Melissa. There was much they had to discuss and he missed her. Living in close quarters over the past years since he had lost his sight had brought them to be incredibly close. They often found themselves finishing each other's sentences or spontaneously humming the same tunes. It was almost as if they had developed, to quote Mellie's favourite pet theorist of the moment, Jung, a form of collective unconsciousness. He felt the tell-tale signs of a grimace tugging at his lips. He paused; life was hard enough without his face contributing to his inner turmoil. He adjusted his muscles. A smile would not come, but blankness he could manage. For now, it would have to do. His face was like a mask; he would be a slave to emotion no more.

'He has some very modern ideas,' the Brigadier persisted, perhaps mistaking the meaning of the mask before him.

However, a short time later, Alasdair had to acknowledge that he was enjoying himself. The Brigadier had made himself scarce after the introductions, allowing Alasdair to talk to Davies on his own terms. Davies had turned out to be an ex-serviceman – the second son of a Welsh farming family invalided out at Mons with a shattered leg. A leg that had been saved but now functioned poorly. He walked with a pronounced limp and relied heavily on a stick. Hearing the unevenness of his walk and the thump of the stick, Alasdair wondered, idly, whether he could still ride. If not, how did he cover the distances over the acreage of the estate?

Davies talked enthusiastically about the estate and outlined a scheme of modernisation using mechanical equipment. Alasdair smiled. A tractor, that is what they needed.

'Look, it may seem that we have plenty of cheap labour now there are so many men unemployed after the war, but it's inefficient, see. The estate should modernise, buy new equipment. Focus on what the output could be. There should be a plan. Are we dairy? Arable? Stock? 'Cos at the moment, see, we are all things to no man.'

'Well, I quite agree,' said Alasdair, impressed. Perhaps this was something he could throw himself into. He had thought planning had been his forte until that blow to the head in the war. 'A plan is a good thing. Why don't you draw one up? Let me have a look at it and we can approach Sir Reginald, Brigadier Ferguson, together.'

'Before you go, I hope you don't mind, but when I heard about your injury from the Brigadier, I had an idea. Look, you—'

'Really!' Melissa jumped in quickly, ever the protective watchdog.

'Trust me. Come along now.' Davies led them into a low barn close to the house, which would once have been part of the extensive stabling for the estate. Melissa sighed as they went in and were presented with the sight of mostly empty stalls. 'I remember before the war ... these stalls were full. Cousins Henry and Richard were crazy about horses.'

Alasdair smiled as the scent of horse and leather sent him back to a time before the war, a time when he had had his sight. A time when he would have been itching to ride out hard and fast.

Davies' voice brought him back before he could get maudlin. 'So you can understand, then, why Her Ladyship loathes the sight of horses now. We just have one shire and a hack for His Lordship and a pony for the trap which I and the servants use when we need. The main stable block has been largely abandoned, some converted for motors. I have some ideas about that too. But come, look.'

He opened a stall and a young golden retriever bounded out. The next thing Alasdair knew, a cold wet nose was pressed into his hand. He reached out and stroked the dog's head, his brow softening as he smiled in delight. 'Her name's Sheba. Not very original name, I know. Came from a litter of good gundog pedigree. I thought she might suit you. She don't take to it, see, the shooting. Hopeless. Hates the loud bangs of the guns.'

'She's not alone then,' muttered Alasdair drily, warming to the hound.

'She's intelligent, though, a good pointer and retriever. We used dogs a lot in the trenches, remember. Good at searching things out, sending messages …'

'Ah, I see!' Melissa exclaimed. 'They mentioned something about this at Moorfields Eye Hospital. They are using dogs in Germany for rehabilitation and guidance for blind ex-servicemen.'

'Don't know about that,' muttered Davies gruffly. 'Using bloody great German Shepherds, oh yes, Alsatians we're meant to call them now, isn't it? Sheba here is a good intelligent dog from these isles. If they're good enough for Wales, they are good enough for me.'

TEN

They walked back to the house, Melissa clinging tightly to Alasdair as she guided the way. It was a cold crisp late autumn morning and their feet crunched as they stepped through the frozen mud of the yard. 'Are you all right, darling?' Alasdair ventured.

'All right? What do you think, you blithering idiot? No I bloody well am not. My cousin is dead and someone in this house killed her, didn't they?'

'Looks like it,' Alasdair muttered morosely, all his good humour over Sheba vanishing.

'Sorry, darling, I didn't mean to snap.'

'Good God, you wouldn't be human if this wasn't affecting you. Listen, let's meet up later, talk some more and compare notes. I must go back and sit in on Maundeville's interviews. I am really worried about the line he is taking. He seems less concerned with a murderer in our midst than he is with spies.'

'Well, I suppose national security takes precedence over everything, but I'd have thought that as we won the war, it was all a bit old hat now.'

'Hardly. I agree that the damage has been done and is

in the past, but we need to protect the future as well, don't forget.'

'Oh true, I hadn't thought of it that way. So many people now want to forget all about the war and just get on with their lives. I'll come and find you before luncheon, shall I? And watch out for George. I am sure he is hiding something.'

Once more ensconced in the wing chair in the library, Alasdair waited for the next interview. He was rather surprised when Sir Simon greeted not a member of the family but rather the hesitant and nervous Agnés Beaume.

What on earth is he playing at? wondered Alasdair. He can't continue with his investigation at the expense of the family. There was a murderer on the loose. They needed to pursue a timeline for the murder and stop fluffing about with the spy angle.

In the smaller of the two drawing rooms, the blue drawing room, Melissa was sitting with Lottie. They sat side by side on one of the chintz sofas. Lottie seemed to be obsessively smoothing one of the cushions. Melissa feared for its nap.

'This is just too terrible. Emma was really sweet. A quiet little mouse. It must be a mistake. Who would want to murder her? Oh!' She gave a squeal and covered her mouth in a theatrical gesture so typical of her cousin. 'Mellie, was she murdered by accident?'

'Accident?' Melissa muttered faintly.

'Yes, you know, instead of someone else?'

'You mean, one of us?' responded Melissa drily.

'Oh gawd.' Her voice rose in response to a hardly credible octave.

'Breath, slowly, calmly, it works,' instructed Melissa. Trust Lottie to resort to hysterics, she thought, and then, considering her own shaking fingers, she chastised herself, put her arm around her cousin and hugged her. They clung together in an increasing soggy embrace. 'Why do you think it must have been an accident?' Melissa asked quietly.

'Well, you see,' Lottie began diffidently. 'She is such an unlikely person to be murdered, isn't she? She was always so quiet, so reserved. She never stood up to anyone. Now, if it had been George, I might have understood it. One can imagine him up to something nefarious, can't one? But Emma?' Her thoughts appeared to drift off.

'What are you thinking? What is it?

'Well, do you know, I have just remembered something. I was at a rather racy party a few months ago. I think it was Poppy Halliday's birthday bash. Her family have a huge house in Chelsea, don't you know? They had hired a fantastic black jazz band for the night and I was desperate to catch them. Well, who should I see across the room but Emma?' She rolled her eyes. 'Yes, Emma, at a party. It was so incongruous that I just goggled at her across the room. By the time I pulled myself together and looked for her, she was gone.'

'Was she with someone?'

'Sorry, I didn't pay any attention. I was so shocked to see her, And' – her voice rose an octave – 'she was wearing a flapper dress, in green, I think. Extraordinary! She looked so different. Quite unlike that abominable creation she was wearing last night.'

'Ah, you noticed that too,' Melissa muttered.

'Yes. But then last night she seemed much more like

herself. Well, how I imagine her to be. I must admit, we had rather lost touch, and then to see her like that. Almost as if … ' She began to cry. 'I—'

The door opened, interrupting whatever it was she was going to say. Melissa turned in exasperation.

'Dear me, dear me, I hope I am not interrupting anything?' It was the vicar.

'Well, how did you get in? I thought we were out of bounds until the murder is solved?' exclaimed Melissa, dabbing a sodden shoulder ineffectively with a handkerchief.

'I am a man of the cloth, my dear. It is my role to attend to those stricken by, by …' he floundered '… unfortunate circumstances.'

'Unfortunate circumstances? The murder of Emma is an unfortunate circumstance?' pealed Lottie and began to sob in earnest.

The vicar crossed the room, pulled up a chair close to Lottie and began to pat her shoulder gently while muttering soothingly, cooing in a low, deep, calming voice. Melissa watched his blond, close-cropped hair, his head dipped as he leaned closer to her cousin. She had to acknowledge that he might actually be quite good at this part of his job. It seemed to be working. Lottie quietened. Melissa rolled her eyes and decided that if Lottie, the former war ambulance driver, was this cut up, she had better check on Rose.

As she left the room, she momentarily diverted into the morning room. From her crocodile day bag, she removed the notebook her aunt had given her, went over to a table and pulled up a chair. She wanted to make notes to report back. She reflected on what her cousin Lottie had said. Could it really be a case of mistaken identity? But, then, did Lottie not realise that the intended victim might be her? Was that what she was trying to say? Melissa shivered. Or could she be the murderer?

She thought about her cousin Lottie. She had somewhat hero-worshipped her – the brave, strong-willed ambulance driver in the war – but they had seemed to drift apart. Lottie had joined a fast set in London, partying every night, and she had had a frightful hangover whenever Melissa had met her. But what traumas had she seen during the war? What was it she wanted perhaps to forget? Lottie never talked about it. Could that trauma turn her into a murderer? No, never. She was her glorious, heroic cousin. She refused to accept otherwise. Remembering Rose, she put the notebook away, straightened her shoulders and left the room.

A search of the other ground-floor rooms revealed the Honourable Rose Tennant in a small sitting room overlooking the kitchen garden. The room was furnished in a feminine style, the overall impression being of pink. Melissa assumed it must be a former housekeeper's office now used by Lady Honor for perhaps accounts or to hide from her husband when necessary. There was a pretty Chippendale escritoire and a couple of seemingly ubiquitous chintz wing armchairs in front of a small fire.

Sitting in one of the chairs was Rose. Melissa could just smell the scent of the pine logs over the cloud of cigarette smoke. There was a full ashtray on the low table in front of her. What must be the cost of all these fires? thought Melissa idly. Turning her attention to Rose, she saw her eyes were red-rimmed from crying. At least here was someone who truly mourned Emma. 'Oh, Rose, I have been looking for you. I wanted to check you were coping with all this.

You came down with Emma, didn't you?'

Rose sniffed, produced a delicate, lace handkerchief, quite in contrast to the robust games mistress Melissa saw before her, and then gazed at Melissa, her eyes filling. 'Yes, she and George had planned to come along together then I cadged a lift. Emma was very kind about it, but George was beastly. I know it was silly of me to push pursuing him, but I am getting desperate.'

Tears began to drip. So much for mourning Emma; mourning her lack of engagement to George more like – this nasty thought crossed Melissa's mind. She squashed it and turned a sympathetic face to Rose. 'So you all came down together?'

'No, I came with Emma. George insisted, in the end, on coming down on his own.'

'They both have cars?' Melissa was amazed. George she could understand, but Emma as well? She had thought they were broke. The money was all on her own side of the family.

'Yes, I think so. Emma's is a very snazzy roadster.'

Melissa parked that fact for later. 'How did she seem on the journey down?'

'She was subdued but fidgety, absolutely refused to engage in proper conversation. I began to think I had upset her as well, so kept my mouth shut for most of the journey. Normally she is so charming; we often meet up when she is not working.'

'Working? Gosh, I have lost touch with her. What was she doing?'

'Well, I say working, I am not sure she is – was – getting paid for it, but then she does – did – have that snazzy car.

This is hard, isn't it? I can't believe she is gone!' She began to cry again.

Melissa's heart softened. Perhaps Rose had, after all, felt something for her cousin. Who was she to criticise this stranger when she didn't even know her cousin had had a job?

'Yes, it is terrible, but anything we know might be useful to finding out who did it. So what was this job?'

'Oh, something to do with refugees, I think, maybe a charity. She was very enthusiastic, but I tended to stop listening – she had so many hard-luck stories to tell about them.'

Melissa back-tracked her opinions; perhaps the Honourable Rose was suited to George after all. There seemed to be a distinct lack of compassion about her. 'Have you had a chance to talk to George since it happened?'

'No, he seems to be avoiding me.' Rose groaned, dabbing her eyes. 'My mother will kill me if I let another potential husband slip through my fingers.' She must have realised what she had said and how it might be construed so turned away from Melissa's prying eyes and began to sob, rather too theatrically for Melissa's liking.

Realising there was little more to be got from her at the moment and having run out of sympathy, Melissa stood up, muttering, 'I think I'll just go and look for him then.'

She began a systematic search of all the ground-floor rooms. Not finding him there, she rang for the butler. A short while later, a very flustered Smithers burst into the room, in a manner quite unlike his usual sonorous decorum. 'You rang, m'lady?'

'Yes, I am looking for George. Have you seen him?'

'No, m'lady, but I think he went out shooting.'

'Out shooting? But doesn't he know there is a murder investigation going on?'

'Yes, but he was told he wouldn't be needed until this afternoon.'

'Well honestly—' began Melissa.

'M'lady?'

'Yes?' Melissa looked up and stared into the face of the butler, startled by his tone.

'I was just going to apprise Her Ladyship. There seems to have been another accident. Below stairs.'

ELEVEN

'You find Her Ladyship and I'll go and find out what's happening.' Melissa, grateful for her sensible brogues, fairly belted out of the billiard room. She ran into the hallway and then into the dining room. The servants' quarters and kitchens were in a sort of half basement wing extending beyond and at right angles to one side of the house. The quickest access was via some circular stairs down from the dining room. The food came up on a dumb waiter; the staff by the stairs.

She pulled open the heavy oak door almost hidden by the matching oak panelling. Only the door knob gave the game away. It was lined with the almost mandatory green baize. She practically flew down the stairs. She could hear raised voices and ran down the long stone-flagged corridor, past the butler's pantry and rooms, the servants' hall and then into the main kitchen. All was in uproar. In the centre of the room was a rather corpulent, red-faced, middle-aged constable, nearly shouting to make himself heard over the cacophony of noise from the agitated servants who were crowding around him.

Melissa viewed the scene and then clapped her hands.

All faces turned to her, their expressions a mixture of excitement, fear and pain. 'Constable, what has happened?'

'The maid, Missus. She's dead.'

'Dead? How? When?'

'In boot room there.' The constable jerked his head in the room's direction.

Before he could say more, Melissa turned and marched into the small room that once would have been the domain of the boot boy and the footmen. Now it was just an odd jobs room. Lying slumped in the corner of the poorly lit room was the outline of a female body, her back to the door. Protruding from her back was a large silver-handled knife. Melissa noted in passing it was from the upstairs silver service and still beautifully polished, glinting in the light from the open door. The sharp, cloying smell of blood filled the small room. Melissa suddenly felt sick, covered her mouth with her hand and stepped away, back over the threshold.

Taking a number of deep breaths to steady herself, she called the constable, instructed him to guard the room and to let no one else in and ran back down the corridor up the stairs to the hall and to the door of the library. She hammered on it with her fist and flung the door open.

Maundeville half rose from his chair, the man of action; the woman in the chair before him turned around to stare. It was the Countess de Orleon. She arched one eyebrow at the interruption. Alasdair, in his seat by the fire, moved his head from side to side as if straining to hear the cause of the interruption. Godfrey Greenwood sat still, his eyes wide. It was like the so fashionable Tableau Vivant, staged ad nauseam at local events. They were all captured in Melissa's sharp gaze in one moment.

'Quick,' Melissa gasped. 'There has been another murder. One of the maids is dead. In the servants' quarters. Boot room.'

Maundeville, with one look at Melissa, barked, 'Show me.' As he left the room, he was yelling for Greenwood to follow him and for the Countess to wait.

Melissa led them to the hall and opened another heavy oak door, again nearly concealed by the oak panelling. It also led to the servants' area, and she ran before them down the circular stairs. This side, the corridor was shorter, and they were soon at the boot room.

Maundeville looked in, swore and then took over. He sent the constable for the doctor, although, as he said, there was no doubt that she was dead and had been for some time. He carefully turned the body over and the victim was revealed to be little Meg, the maid. Was she the last one left that still lived in?

Melissa sighed heavily, and Maundeville cast a questioning glance at her. 'Lady Honor told me earlier that Meg insisted she knew something about the death of Miss Ferguson. Apparently she was in the kitchen when the murder occurred.'

'What? Why didn't anyone tell me?'

'Well, presumably she told the constable. He was questioning the servants.' Melissa was stung into retorting. She had been asked to spy, and she had done so. It was hardly her fault if they didn't give her time to report what she had found out.

It was Maundeville's turn to sigh. 'Well we can do nothing about it now until the constable returns. Is there a key to this room?'

Mrs Smithers was normally a round, jolly Hampshire Hog (as locals were known), the housekeeper-cum-cook and redoubtable wife of the butler. She approached Maundeville and took a key off the chatelaine ring that hung from her waist. She was crying and wiped her tears on her apron before returning to stand with the other servants, as though safety in numbers would protect them.

'Good.' Maundeville nodded his thanks. 'I'll lock it. You, Mrs Charters, will come with us.'

Where she had just led, Melissa found herself following Maundeville and taking up the rear, Greenwood behind her. When they arrived at the library, it was to find it empty except for a red-faced and agitated Alasdair.

'What the hell is going on?' he began. 'The Countess has done a bunk and left me here.'

'Not now,' drawled Maundeville. 'Greenwood, can you go and check on the whereabouts of everyone? Still, at least we can cross off any visitors from last night.'

'No, you can't.' said Melissa. 'The vicar is here.'

'Good Gad, this lark is beginning to try my patience. Go, Greenwood, and find out who is here and has been here all morning for a start.'

Melissa looked over at Alasdair. He was still flushed and clearly agitated, frowning in his attempt to hear through silence. She went over and took his hand. 'It's all right, Alasdair. I am here. Well, actually, it is not all right. Meg, the upstairs maid, is dead. Stabbed.'

Alasdair relaxed back in his chair. 'Same MO as the other then.'

'MO?'

'Modus operandi. Don't need to teach you your Latin, do I?'

'Ah, method of operation?'

'Absolutely.' Alasdair beamed, almost like a school teacher over his favourite pupil. She did love him. She squeezed his hand, relief flooding through her at the comfort of his touch, dispelling the urge to cry as the adrenaline, which had followed the shock of Meg's murder, dissipated. The cloying smell of blood seemed to have followed her, settling in her nostrils.

'Look, Maundeville, are you still there?' Alasdair said. 'This looks more and more to me like a family issue. Why don't Melissa and I recce the family, you continue with your investigation and we swap notes?'

Maundeville's expression turned bullish. 'No, no, we will continue as is. I need you in on the interviews.'

Melissa suspected he was the kind of man who did not change his plans lightly. 'Well, someone has to interview the staff. That constable was obviously useless. He allowed Meg to be murdered virtually under his nose.'

'I appreciate that, Melissa, but my investigation could be a matter of national security.'

'Not much good if, in the meantime, we are bumped off one by one,' commented Alasdair drily.

'Oh, all right, you two go and find out what you can. The interview with the Countess is ruined for now anyway. We'll meet up again here, say six o'clock, after tea,' Maundeville conceded with bad grace.

Thankful to be released and bursting with information, Melissa grabbed Alasdair, as he had already leapt athletically out of the chair, and led him out of the room before

Maundeville could change his mind.

'Listen, Mellie, we have to find Brigadier Ferguson. It is his house and this is bloody serious.'

'I agree. Any idea where he is?'

'Well, we have kicked him out of the libraries. What about his study?'

Reginald, Brigadier Ferguson, was indeed in his study. They passed the banker, Bernard Lyon, in the hallway leading to it. He rushed past, not greeting them or even glancing their way, his bald pate gleaming, his overweight form panting with exertion. A slight fragrance hovered in his wake. Something had riled him. Melissa had just time to comment on this before they entered the study. This, she reflected, was a real man's room: a stag's head graced the wall above the wide stone fireplace, and it smelled of old leather and wet dog.

'Good grief!' Brigadier Ferguson exploded. 'What the hell is going on? The world has gone mad. Melissa, go find your aunt. Alasdair, come and sit down, we need to talk.'

Melissa glanced quickly at her uncle. Had he forgotten Alasdair's limitations in his agitation? She led Alasdair to a chair close to her uncle's desk, putting his hand on the chair back. Reginald glared at her. 'Go, girl, don't dawdle.'

Shrugging, a useless gesture as it was lost on Alasdair, she left.

'What is it bothering you, sir?' Alasdair asked softly.

'What, aside from bloody murder you mean?'

'Well, I agree this is not the normal house party. What the hell is going on? Who are all these people and why are they here?'

'Well, Maundeville and his crowd are here 'cos he

80

asked me. We fought together, don't you know. He wanted somewhere quiet and neutral. I explained that I had the family down, but he said that he thought that would help muddy the waters. God knows what he's up to.'

'Yes, well, the waters are definitely muddied now, sir. With murder.'

Brigadier Ferguson continued as if he hadn't heard. 'I s'pose you just passed Bernard in the hall? Face like thunder, I expect.' Alasdair opened his mouth, but Brigadier Ferguson got in first. 'Damn and blast, forgot your eyesight. Shouldn't have sent Melissa away. Sorry, damn fool, old-fashioned, don't you know. Wanting to protect the little lady. Should have known better. Like my Honor, she's got character, backbone. You knew what you were at when you married her. And she didn't get shot of you when you came back crippled. Many would have done, you know. Yes, a fine woman.'

Get to the point, man, Alasdair's brain shouted.

'Yes, she has a strong will and that is what this place needs and that is what I got you down here for. To see if you'd both consider making a go of it. Had to invite them all or it would have looked funny.'

More like spares in case we refused, thought Alasdair cynically. Brigadier Ferguson seemed to have temporarily run out of steam, lost in apparent reflection. An increasing tendency, Alasdair noticed. In the momentary silence, Alasdair risked, 'And Bernard? Why is he here?'

'Well now, that is a rather odd thing. You see, when the boys …' He coughed. 'Er … went off one by one, I sort of flunked it. Honor insisted I took advice, so I asked about at the club, and it was generally agreed he was the man.'

'The man for what?' Alasdair was losing patience. Didn't he realise that there were two dead bodies about the house?

'Finance, dear boy, finance. Invested with him and I made a packet. My sons died, mown down in their prime while I made a fortune. Unreal, unhealthy, don't like it.'

'Well, you would be the first man I have met who complained of getting rich.'

Brigadier Ferguson continued as if he hadn't heard. 'Avoided him after that. Didn't feel right, profiting while our boys died. Then, out of the blue, he telephones, wants to come down and see me. Well, I thought we had enough on our plate this weekend, but he wouldn't take no for an answer. So I thought, well, he can advise me on what I should do, inheritance and all that. But all he wanted to talk about was some poncey scheme. Sounded fishy to me. Besides, I've got enough now. Time to reinvest in the land, the estate, don't you think? But do you know what the odd thing was?'

No, but I am sure you are going to tell me, thought Alasdair.

'He didn't even give me the hard sell. Gave it up far too easily for a money man. Usually like a dog after a rabbit. No, he blathered on about his motor accident, and then all he could talk about was that damned Frog countess. I mean, I ask you. Still could have been worse – if he had been murdered there would have been hell to pay.' He guffawed. 'Sent him off with a right flea in his ear. Frog Countess. Pah!'

TWELVE

'Well, first off, I suggest care with Bernard. Melissa reads the markets to me every day. Now, as you so bluntly stated, I am a cripple, I am not exactly work material, so I need to keep a tight handle on my assets. The markets look very volatile to me. Whereas with your estate, you have a good man there in Davies. He has some intelligent modern ideas. He is drawing some plans up at the moment.'

'There, then, got the bit between your teeth already. That's what I like.'

'Yes, that is all very well, but what are we going to do about these murders?' Alasdair spoke calmly and slowly, not allowing his frustration to show. Sir Reginald, the former Brigadier and man of action, blustered and barked like an army man, but the death of his two sons had taken its toll, Alasdair thought. As a result, he had lost his focus – was all over the place, in fact. His command of situations lost in grief?

There was a discreet knock at the door.

'Come,' yelled the Brigadier.

Smithers entered. 'I wondered if you gentlemen would

be so kind as to gather in the drawing room. I understand that Sir Maundeville wishes to address you all.'

'Well, that is a bit rich, in m'own house too. Still, if we don't want to all be murdered in our beds I s'pose we'd better comply.'

He sounds positively chipper, thought Alasdair, struggling to keep up with the Brigadier's shifting moods. Now what?

'Mr Charters, I have apprised your wife of the situation. She'll be along shortly, sir.'

'Phew. Here, I am Alasdair. This whole thing is getting beastly. Uncle, we need you. Even the men are bordering on hysteria.' Melissa bounced back into the room and touched Alasdair on the arm to let him know where she was.

The Brigadier marched off at a quick-time pace. Alasdair desperately wanted to talk to Melissa and find out what she knew. He also wanted to get his own thoughts in order. Why did he have to be blind? Even taking simple notes was fraught. He needed his typewriter with him; he'd been taught typing at St Dunstan's, but without using a very expensive dictation machine, he had no way of reading any notes that he had typed. Always, always he depended on someone else, and it was this that hurt. Man of action turned to a dependent. He gave a gloomy sigh and then caught hold of Melissa's elbow and they followed behind the Brigadier at a more leisurely pace. Smithers, ever the consummate servant, brought up the rear.

The drawing room was in a state of uproar as they slipped in, close behind the Brigadier. 'Silence,' he bellowed. 'Let's have a bit of decorum. Maundeville, what the devil is going on in my house, man?'

When everyone's ears had stopped ringing, Maundeville opened his mouth to speak, but Bernard Lyon got there first. 'Reginald, this man is refusing to let us leave. Are we to stay here and be picked off one by one? Someone has already tried to run me off the road last night. I could damn well be next.'

'Language, man! Ladies present. We must do all we can to find out what the hell?' He harrumphed. 'The dickens is going on, Maundeville?'

Maundeville began again. 'One murder could have been the work of an itinerant madman, but two murders means that someone in this house is a murderer.' He stared around as if by strength of will he could identify the murderer. All he got was an apparent roomful of rabbits caught in a motor's headlights.

'In order to track the said person down, we will have to interview the lot of you. I have been given until nine o'clock on Monday morning when Scotland Yard will be coming. If we haven't found the person by then, I can assure you that what you are experiencing now is child's play compared to their tactics. So, I suggest that you all remain here until we can sort out a proper system of interviews.'

Melissa saw how he glanced at Alasdair; she wondered what had transpired between the two men. Still, if they were confined to the house and grounds, then at least she and Alasdair could compare notes. She was itching to share her discoveries and wanted to know just what Maundeville had found out.

'Well, mes amis, I for one have nothing to hide. This business just adds a frisson of excitement to what could have been a rather dull weekend,' said the Countess.

'Speak for yourself, Madame. We were looking forward to a most enjoyable weekend with family.' Lottie's blue eyes dripped ice. The Countess shrugged and looked away. An awkward silence stretched.

'Has Colonel Manders left yet?' Maundeville ventured.

'Yes, sir, I believe he left after dinner last night. He wanted to get back to barracks,' Greenwood replied.

'Ah yes, you are correct as usual. Shame, I could have used him. All right, we will continue with the interviews in the library but starting with the family. Major and Mrs Charters, we will start with you. Greenwood, you can take notes.'

They all trooped back into the library. Greenwood was again conveniently sent out on an errand.

'Look, you were right, Alasdair. I should have listened. What I need you two to do now is to sit in with the house party, ask questions, listen in and then we can report back. Without Manders, I dare not trust anyone, not even Greenwood, and neither should you. We will meet up as arranged at six o'clock this evening and compare notes. Anything I should know now?'

'Well, I hate to say this, but you should question George. He definitely knows something. Oh and Cousin Emma was working for a charity with refugees. Is this yet another link to the war?'

'Good grief, Alasdair. Your wife is a positive bloodhound. I might just recruit her myself after this. Well done.'

'And the maid, Meg, did know something or thought she did. Lady Honor might know about it, but I doubt it. Apparently she does not listen to servants. You'll need to question all the servants. That constable was obviously worse than useless.'

'Bit out of his depth, I suspect,' muttered Alasdair. 'Bet all he usually has to deal with is a bit of pig rustling.'

'Pig rustling?'

'New Forest, commoners' rights, animals allowed to roam. History lesson anyone?' He grinned.

'All right, smarty, forget the history. Just let us get this killer. Could everyone here physically have committed the murders? Sir Simon, what did the doctor say?'

'I still need to speak to him. The constable said he has a complicated delivery over at Lyndhurst. The living come before the dead, but you have a point. Someone knew precisely where to slide the knife in to kill.'

'True, sir. The ribs are there for a reason. We saw that in the trenches – they saved many a man in a bayonet charge.' The door opened and Greenwood entered.

'All right, I have obtained lists of staff and guests from Lady Honor. We can now proceed, I think?'

'Indeed, change of plan,' said Maundeville. 'Let us start with the servants. Fetch Smithers first. We had better do this in order of precedence. Don't want the soup poisoned.'

THIRTEEN

Alasdair and Melissa made their way back to the drawing room. Alasdair stopped abruptly and sighed, almost causing Melissa to stumble, but, used to his foibles, she remained still and silent, giving him space. He checked his Braille wristwatch. 'So much time has been lost. We are floundering. My mind is racing. It's all too much. I need to slow down. When we get to the drawing room, put me in a corner and leave me there a while. I need to think.'

'Are you sure you wouldn't like to go into a quieter room?'

'Yes.'

This terse comment was the first inclination Melissa had had that he was rattled. It chilled her far more than any other word could have done. That sense of dread that she had been pushing away into a dark corner crept its way insidiously to the surface and wrapped its coils around her psyche. She shivered.

'Melissa?' He was too damned perceptive.

'I'm fine.' She was pleased it came out without a quiver in her voice, 'These corridors are like ice. Here, we are outside the small pink sitting room. Let's pop in here for a moment.'

She led Alasdair to a pink chintz boudoir chair. He sat, his long lithe frame looking incongruous surrounded by such femininity. In spite of her fear, Melissa smiled. With him here, she could cope with anything. He was her rock, but, in turn, since he had become blind, she was like a tigress defending her cub; she would fight to the death to protect him. She gave him a few moments to settle, pulling up another chair so that she could sit opposite him and observe his beloved face.

The silence extended and then he spoke. 'The priority here is your safety.' He gave the semblance of a grin. 'What would I do without you? You are my rock. You must promise me you will be sensible.'

'Stop it, Alasdair, you really are frightening me.' She wound her arms around her body, suddenly cold again. She glanced at the fireplace. The earlier fire was almost out. Feeling guilty, she rose and, grabbing a poker, raked over the embers for a glow and threw another log on. She supposed living in a forest had some advantages. 'I intend to be sensible, I assure you.'

'Good. This is no longer a game. A game of spies. This is now murder – two murders – and the perpetrator will not stop until they feel safe. We have to find out their motive. Why Emma and why the maid? What was it they knew? I will listen but you, my darling, need to use your eyes. Observe everything, miss nothing, and tell no one, only me.'

'What about Maundeville?'

'Me first. Trust no one, not even family.' He lapsed

into silence. 'It's just I cannot get a handle on this. I can sense evil, real evil here, but the source? I thought it was the Countess, and it may well be. But there is something else, something hidden, in a dark corner. How well do you know your family?'

'Really?' Melissa snapped but then paused. 'OK, to be strictly true, not a lot over the last umpteen years. I saw a bit of the girls early in the war but then lost touch. We wrote, of course, but did not meet up. Of George, I know only what I have been told by aunts and my mother, and I suppose that may not have been very accurate. He could have been up to anything. It was as children that we knew each other – summer holidays together and that sort of thing.'

'So that is what we need to find out. Who or what are they, where they have been, what they have done? Questions, questions and more questions.'

'But why should they tell us?'

'Why not? I am a blind cripple and you are a fluffy aristo.' He laughed at her snort of derision. 'Now come over here and give me a kiss. I need some restoration before we greet the mob.'

A good five minutes later she opened the door of the green drawing room to pandemonium. It appeared that anyone who had a voice was shouting. She weaved her way through the throng with Alasdair securely on her arm and placed him in front of a vacant chair in a corner of the room. He felt for the back, turned and sat down. With a quick squeeze of his shoulder, she waded into the furore.

It was Brigadier Ferguson who brought decorum to the room, bellowing, 'Order, order, you lot! Get a grip. Let us give Maundeville the respect he deserves. We need him.'

'But we need out. If we are not to be m-murdered, picked off one by one,' stuttered Bernard. 'Two dead already and I have been run off the road. It will be me next, I tell you.'

'So you keep telling us. Stay calm, man,' the Brigadier replied, his voice laced with disdain. 'We men should be setting an example for the women.'

There was an exaggerated sigh from Lottie. One look from Brigadier Ferguson and she turned it into a cough. 'Now, let us proceed to help Maundeville the best we can. I expect all of you to co-operate. Lady Honor has given me a list of everyone who is staying at the house. Other than the vicar' – he rounded to look at him, and the vicar coloured – 'who else have you seen visiting today?'

'Well, I have been shooting with Arthur Baggeley. I invited him in for a coffee and a snifter,' George drawled.

The Brigadier sighed. 'Well then, that means that everyone who sat down to dinner last night may have also been here this morning at the time of the murder.'

'What about that colonel?' asked George.

'Ah, yes, Colonel Manders returned to HQ after dinner last night, so we can eliminate him as he had gone before the first murder.' Maundeville had slipped into the room unnoticed. 'Now,' he continued. 'You all stay here and I will resume interviews in the library. I have just had a very interesting chat with Smithers. He, at least, seems to have a grasp of things below stairs. We'll start with you, George, shall we?' It sounded like a threat.

George shrugged. Melissa frowned; he looked far too casual about it for someone who, she was sure, was hiding something. If she didn't feel in her heart of hearts that he was incapable of murder, he would be top of her list of suspects.

'Listen, I tell you I want off. This is no place to stay! I am not going to be murdered,' said Bernard.

'O dear, mon vieux, are you really so … what is the word? Spineless. Come, stay close to me and I will protect you.' The Countess sauntered up to Bernard, took his arm and led him over to the window, away from the throng. Melissa noticed as she swayed across the room that she was wearing a startlingly red chiffon day dress, with high matching heels, quite the wrong thing to be wearing in the morning at a country house. Melissa herself was in brogues, a tweed skirt and silk blouse. She shivered again. She wondered if she could slip upstairs and grab a cardigan. She looked round and grinned at her cousin Lottie; she was just about to make her way over when Lady Honor caught Melissa's arm and pulled her away.

Alasdair, meanwhile, sat still in the corner by the window, his back to the light, and listened. Was it possible to become invisible? The waves of expensive perfume wafted over in his direction.

'Do not speak to me in that way.' The voice low and indignant.

'Well stop making an ass of yourself, mon cher, or is that your intention? Your little … what is the word? Ploy?'

'Quiet, we may be overheard.'

Alasdair assumed it was himself being indicated, but, of course, he could not see.

'The blow on the head that blinded him probably addled his wits too. Even his wife abandons him whenever she can.'

'Don't be daft, woman, you can never tell. And he is thick with Maundeville. You can drop all that French simpering. It is wasted on me, as you should well know.'

'Huh, Maundeville! He is probably just suffering from the suppressed guilt. That is the speciality of you English, suppression, is it not?'

'Yes, well, you will know all about that – quite the expert, my dear.'

They moved away, still bickering, and Alasdair was left to his contemplation. He wondered what Melissa was up to. Abandoning him, as if that were true. He shifted, uncomfortable in his chair. Had she listened to him? Did she understand? She was reckless, he knew only too well. After all, she had married him. She an aristocrat and he newly down from Cambridge, no career in mind, rescued, he thought, by the war. He would shine, get a promotion and a career sorted. That was a laugh. Instead of the dashing soldier, she had been lumbered with a useless lump. It couldn't be much fun for her; perhaps the Countess was right. He could hardly blame Melissa if she left him. He grimaced, but then she had not. Why? Duty? Honour? He couldn't imagine he was much fun. He needed to pull himself together, make a go of this, but first he had to figure out these murders for both their sakes.

Melissa was listening patiently to Lady Honor once again; she had handed Melissa a list of all the guests and the staff and then drawn her away to the side of the room. 'I only wish I could remember what it was that Meg was twittering about.'

Melissa turned her aside and said urgently and in a low voice, 'Shh, Meg was probably murdered for what she heard, and if the murderer hears she told you anything, you could be next.'

'Don't be silly! Surely not?'

'Yes, listen to me – if you remember, tell only me. Do you understand?' She looked into her aunt's eyes, hard and long, until she saw the wobble of fear appear on her lips. 'Yes, now you realise we have a lunatic among us.'

She nodded.

'Can you remember nothing?'

'No,' Lady Honor said crisply. 'I sort of stopped listening as I was thrown back into thinking about the boys and yet ...' She tapped her chin. 'Why did I do that?'

She frowned and Melissa could see her trying hard to recall the moment. 'You know, why Meg should be rabbiting on about it, I have no idea, but I have this feeling ... That's it! There was something about Germans or Germany.'

FOURTEEN

elissa pulled on her aunt's arm and steered her
away to a quieter part of the room. 'Germany?
Really? This is serious. You realise Maundeville
is looking for a spy?'

Lady Honor's eyes grew round, and she raised a shaking
hand to her mouth. 'Yes.'

Melissa nodded. 'Remember, tell no one – only me
or Maundeville.' She glanced at her wristlet watch; it was
nearly twelve o'clock. Looking at her aunt's colour, she
deliberately attempted to distract her. 'What is happening
about lunch, Aunt?'

'Well, it will have to be a bit of a mess. I have ordered
coffee and sandwiches. Some cold cuts and boiled potatoes.
In the dining room, a sort of cold buffet. Not ideal, but it
will have to do.'

As if on cue, Smithers reappeared and announced that
a light luncheon was available in the dining room. Melissa
hung back and waited until the room emptied. Lady
Honor, ever the concerned hostess, had bustled ahead of
the throng.

Melissa approached Alasdair, who was still sitting on

the chair by the window. 'Alone at last. Are you starving or shall we have a bit of a chat about things?' She pulled up a chair and sat opposite him, but before she could begin, the door flew open and George crashed into the room.

'What the hell did you say to Maundeville, Melissa? He was positively bloody. Practically accused me of murder!'

Melissa stood up abruptly, poised for quite what she could not have said, but for action anyway. George marched over and sat in her chair and then slumped down, all his fight gone. With a sigh, she brought up another chair.

'Not just me, George. You have been behaving very oddly.'

'Oddly? My sister is dead!' He coughed, and large fat tears ran down his face.

Alasdair pulled out a clean handkerchief and handed it to him. George gave a double take but did not comment. Melissa smiled wryly; yes, they did all think that Alasdair was a fool.

'OK, I admit to you, I was hoping to touch the banker, Lyon, for some dosh if I couldn't get any out of Old Uncle Reggie, but that was it.'

'What for?'

'What do you mean what for? To use, to live on, to invest. Any bally use you can think of that you need dosh for.' He glanced at Melissa. 'We don't all have a trust fund, and he isn't short of a bob or two, is he?' He tipped his head towards Alasdair. 'I'm from the poor side of the family. Remember?'

Melissa thought of the starving masses, of ex-soldiers begging on the streets, and she had to repress a stringent retort. 'Well, we have to be careful, but yes, you are right we are not broke.'

'And nor are you likely to be. I can see the way the land lies down here with you.'

'Oh, hardly—' Melissa began.

George snorted and pulled an incredulous face.

'Well, what have you done with yours?' she asked. 'Dosh, I mean. I thought you worked in the government during the war.'

'Yes, for a pittance. Look, motors are the future, I have a chance to invest in a nice little motor business. I just need the capital.'

'But why did you think Bernard Lyon would lend you the money?'

'Oh, I wasn't hoping he'd lend as such, more of a permanent loan.'

'But why on earth would you think he'd do that?' Melissa broke in. 'Bankers are hardly renowned for their generosity.'

'Ah well, that was where Emma was going to come in – she had been seeing quite a bit of Bernard. I suspect she had hopes in that direction in the beginning, but then she took against him.'

'Any idea why?' asked Alasdair softly.

'No, not really, but she intimated it was serious and called him a vile little sewer rat. Quite extreme for dear Emma.' He blew noisily into the handkerchief. Melissa was actually beginning to feel sorry for George, and then she remembered the loan. Or could it be called blackmail? And there were the flashy cars. She turned to him, stalling the hand that had reached out to rest on his shoulder in sympathy.

'So where did you get the money for the cars you and Emma already own?'

'Oh, spiffing motors, aren't they both? Mellie, you must take a turn in the motor that Emma drove down.'

In the face of Melissa's incredulity, he rushed on. 'It's OK, stop worrying. They are on loan. I am working as a salesman for a showroom, but I have the chance to get in on the business end. Emma and I have been pootling about in the cars to weekends like this and drumming up sales.'

'And has it worked?'

'Oh yes, they are both top-hole motors. The little roadster Emma brought down would be just the ticket for you, Mellie. Why don't you come out and look at it now?'

George's eyes were alight with fervour, and Melissa had the strong suspicion that she was not going to be let off lightly from his clearly superior sales technique. Alasdair reached out and took her hand and squeezed it. 'What do you think, darling? Shall we have a look at it after lunch?'

'Great stuff, see you about two o'clock by the front door then. Coming into lunch, you two?' George sprang from his seat and bounded like a wet puppy across yet another Aubusson rug to the door.

'Well, that cheered him up,' commented Alasdair drily.

'Yes, but what about it? That stuff about Bernard Lyon – it sounded to me like blackmail,' Melissa huffed.

'Possibly, but over what?'

'She worked for that charity with refugees, maybe she came across something illegal or underhand.'

'Spies, perhaps?' Alasdair raised an eyebrow.

'Oh, I think that is a bit of a leap. Trouble is, we are not going to find out about it now, are we? Whatever it is, she has been silenced. And talking about silenced, Aunt Honor thought Meg, the parlour maid, was talking about Germans or Germany when she was hysterical last night.'

'Good God, and she has only thought to mention it just now?'

'Well, she is just not the same as she was. Losing the boys has devastated her. She is so old-fashioned in many ways, clinging to the old values. She certainly has not updated her ideas about servants. Positively Edwardian, my dear. Which is why, I suppose, she wasn't listening to her properly.'

'Well, let's grill George some more after lunch, although I have a bad feeling about his selling prowess.'

'Bad?' She registered the look on his face. 'Ah, too good, you mean. You might have to part with some dosh for a top-hole motor?' She chuckled, then sobered. 'And we haven't even had a chance to talk to your reporter chappie.'

'What about your cousin Lottie and the Honourable Rose?'

'Trouble is, I am beginning to suspect everyone. All Rose wants is to nobble George in the matrimony stakes, and it seems all Lottie wants, to quote George, is enough dosh to marry your reporter.'

'I tell you who else might be interesting – the Countess's companion, Agnés.'

'What, that mousy thing? She wouldn't hurt anyone, surely.'

'Yes, but she might creep around and pick things up. Mice like the crumbs from the table, don't they?'

FIFTEEN

Despite Lady Honor's protestations, Melissa and Alasdair enjoyed a very substantial lunch. Perhaps not quite the formal three courses that might be the norm at a country house weekend; however, they were quite full enough and feeling quite mellow after quaffing an excellent white wine with cold ham, boiled potatoes, assorted other boiled vegetables and an excellent shape with tinned fruit for pudding.

The company round the table was sombre, quite unlike the expected weekend joviality, even with the plentiful wine. Melissa glanced across at Lottie, usually the life and soul of any party. She looked unusually wan; her clear luminescent skin seemed pulled tight over her cheekbones and there were dark circles forming under those cerulean-blue eyes. Under scrutiny, she looked up, caught Melissa's interrogative look, gave an almost infinitesimal shake of her head which was ambiguous, and then looked down, continuing to push the bright pink shape around her plate. For once, she seemed content with silence.

Next to her, Henry Blake, an empty plate and a full wine glass before him, almost seemed to crackle with suppressed energy. He was alert, reminding Melissa of a hound after the scent. Now he would be a good witness to question. She would be willing to bet there was not much that he missed. Then she reflected that he was probably composing his copy now, exposing her family to scandal. Unless, of course, he was the murderer.

She bit her lip; this was so difficult. She looked up and saw that she was being scrutinised, in turn, by Henry. He nodded at her and gave what appeared to be a genuine smile. She grinned back, deciding to take it at face value.

'Do you and Lottie fancy a walk later?' she asked.

'Lotts has a headache, but if she feels better then yes. Give us an hour. Actually, I'll come anyway. See you in an hour. Back of the house?'

'Can you make it in two hours, just to be on the safe side? Let's meet by the stables. Not too late, though, as it will get dark early, don't forget.'

'Not afraid of the dark are you, Melissa?' His sardonic voice grated for a moment.

'No,' interrupted Alasdair. 'But she should be, and so should you all.'

'Not you?'

'The dark holds no fears for me.' Alasdair's voice was bitter. 'It is just what people do in it that needs to be feared.'

Lottie pushed her chair back and rushed from the room.

'A sick headache – she has had them since the war. Excuse me, she will need help.' Henry rose and followed her out.

Left alone with just the servants, Melissa glanced up at Smithers. 'Coffee will be in the drawing room, Mrs Charters.'

She squeezed Alasdair's arm. 'Come on, Alasdair, they want to clear. I hope the staff can make some inroads into the food that is left. Looks like we were last in, and soon we have an appointment with a car.'

The drawing room was empty too – the coffee pot, cups and saucers standing on a silver tray. It looked like few people had bothered. The fug of cigarette smoke had almost cleared. Melissa wondered where everyone was. Locked in their rooms for an afternoon siesta? She contemplated how Maundeville was getting on. Clearly nothing was going to happen quickly.

In silence, they had a quick coffee as they had time to kill before their appointed time with George. On leaving the room, they found Thomas, Alasdair's valet, hovering, and he was dispatched to fetch warm clothes. On his return, he subtly led Alasdair to the downstairs toilet. It had been constructed from what must have been an extra boot room or coat room, and Melissa silently commended her aunt and uncle for their adherence to modern plumbing. That, at least, seemed to have been updated throughout the house. She slipped on her coat and walked out the front door, standing in the porch, stamping her feet to ward off the cold.

She turned, hearing Alasdair's voice, and then paused. Of course, she thought. Thomas should have all the gossip from the servants' hall. She stepped from the porch and began pacing up and down on the gravel at the front of the house. There was a perfect turning circle around an island bed which was looking rather sad in the autumn. It had a central planted area containing a majestic classical urn on a matching tall Doric column planted with ivy. The bed itself limped on with desultory heather and lavender; it looked neglected. The bed was surrounded by grass, a rich green after all the rain they had had that autumn.

When she heard the sound of a car coming round the side of the house, she swung around in anticipation. There in front of her was a spiffing green motor. It didn't look too big to Melissa; George had the top down and she could see that it would just about hold four people at a pinch. He drew up in front of her, kept the car idling, ran round and opened the passenger door for her.

What then followed was one of the most thrilling times of her life. They sped down the long driveway and out onto the open road. A short way along, George turned the car around at a junction, pulled in and got out. 'Come on, cuz, your turn at the wheel.'

'Me?' she squeaked.

'Well, it is not going to be that chump of a husband of yours, is it? If Emma could do it, so can you, in spades.'

'Really? Don't I need lessons? Permission?'

'Only from me. Come on, in you hop.'

Slowly at first, and then, as she gained confidence, a little faster, always with a wary eye for animals on the road. The New Forest was common land and donkeys, ponies and cattle as well as pigs roamed freely there. She hated to think what would happen if one hit an animal in a car. They certainly seemed disinclined to move out of the way when she came across them. It involved much braking and swerving. Still, she was able to gambol along happily with the wind in her hair, and she shrieked with delight when George instructed her to go through the water splash at speed, splashing them both and requiring the use of the windscreen wipers afterwards. She was pleased to navigate it safely, especially as George said that cars often got stuck there. The trick, apparently, was enough speed.

However, forty minutes later, she drove rather sedately but confidently up the drive and turned in front of the house. She had hoped to grill George some more about Emma, but between concentrating on the new skill and the thrill of the new and unknown, she just let it go to live in the moment. Looking across at George, he too seemed to have forgotten his cares; his eyes shone and his face was flushed with the wind whipping his hair. He suddenly looked very young, almost vulnerable. Was this the face of a ruthless blackmailer and potential murderer? No, she refused to believe it. She waved as she steered the car around the island bed.

Alasdair and Thomas were sitting on a stone bench in front of one of the bay windows. 'I say, Mrs Charters, you look top hole behind the wheel,' Thomas exclaimed, getting up.

Alasdair groaned. 'Enjoying yourself, my dear?'

'Alasdair, it is quite glorious. It is essential that we have it. George, do your stuff,' she commanded with a grin.

George entered into the role with gusto, his enthusiasm making his face appear boyish, all trace of his usual sardonicism wiped away. 'She really is a beauty, Alasdair. New model Austin 7, perfect for a lady to handle. She did handle well, didn't she, Mellie?'

'Oh yes, George, delightfully.'

Alasdair sighed and bowed to the inevitable. His wife was thoughtful, caring and had a lot to put up with, especially with him as a husband. She deserved a treat. He haggled with George for long enough to satisfy all parties, but George had not finished yet.

'Righty ho, Alasdair, come on, you can do the honours with the starting handle.'

He showed Melissa how to set the starter and the choke, and then he led Alasdair to the starting handle at the front. 'You too, Mellie, you both need to be able to do it, and your valet as well, I guess.' They then each had a go at starting the car with the starting handle. To Alasdair's surprise, it was easier than he had thought.

'What happens if the motor goes wrong?' Alasdair said.

'There will be a local firm near here. I'll look them up. I assume you will mainly motor up and down between here and your flat. I'll make a list of garages on the route. I suggest you join the Automobile Association – they are a great font of news and can help out in a crisis. Good for alerting you to police bikes.'

'Why?' Melissa asked, confused.

'Speeding.' George nodded sagely. 'You think you won't but I bet you will.' He laughed.

'Accidents?' queried Alasdair.

'Get insurance. I suggest Lloyds.'

'Hmm.' Alasdair scratched his chin. 'So would Lyon have been insured, do you think, for his motor accident?'

'Oh yes. Only an idiot would not spend the money. Of course, if he crashes regularly it would cost him a packet, but then he is rich enough not to have to claim if necessary, isn't he?'

'Is he, do you think?'

'Oh, yes, rich as Croesus. Lent money all over the place

and is now calling it in. Invested in munitions and steel during the war.'

'You seem to know a remarkable amount about him.'

'Well, I am not quite as stupid as I appear either – bit like you, as it happens. I want to get this motor business off the ground, and I am going to be successful. I just know it. So it pays to do your homework.'

'And Emma was helping with that?' Alasdair could not stop the tone of accusation creeping into his voice.

'So I thought, but she had gone all quiet and moody and very unforthcoming on the dirt.' George scuffed his feet.

'Are you sure? If you are holding anything back, it could be dangerous.'

'No, dammit, I'm not.' The foot scuffing got louder.

'Does he have any interests in Germany? I would have thought it was also ripe for plucking.' Alasdair decided to risk throwing this in.

'No. Word on the markets is that Germany is finished, but now I think about it, you could be right about Lyon. There was some talk about investments before the war. Of course, it would be prudent to keep that quiet, wouldn't go down well with the families of the war dead. Not quite British to profit from the war. But to be seen to be fleecing the Germans might be acceptable.' George's feet became still.

'Is that why he took an interest in Emma's refugees?' Melissa asked.

'Don't think so. I assumed it was to toady up to the establishment. After all, those of us that sat out the war are not viewed too favourably by them on the whole.'

Melissa hadn't thought of it that way; she wondered if that was one of the causes of George's barbed protective shell. 'And what of a wife to support you in business?' she murmured, pushing the boat out.

'Not if I can help it, I need no distractions.'

'But surely Rose's parents will have funds you can tap into?'

'Look, Rose was Emma's idea. She is a nice girl but a wet fish, positively dripping, and her father is a pompous ass that will turn up his nose at a suitor in trade, I can assure you. It won't work.' He leant forward, his face fierce. 'So don't meddle.'

Melissa backed away, momentarily frightened by his intensity, but did that make him a killer?

'Remember, Mellie, and you too, Alasdair, I appreciate you buying the car but don't interfere with my plans. I am warning you.'

SIXTEEN

'Phew, that was a bit intense.'

Alasdair laughed. 'Well, you did presume to comment on his love life. That was a bit intrusive even for a cousin.'

'Oh, do you really think so? It is 1922, after all.'

'Yes, I do, now come on. Let us see if we can get this car started on our own and you can drive us round to the stables. Thomas, can you squash in the back?'

Melissa watched with pride as Alasdair ran his hand down the side of the car round the bonnet and then bent to the starting handle. With two goes, it was started. He returned the same way, found the door handle and sat himself in. 'Drive on, Jeeves.' He turned and grinned at her.

'Um, shouldn't that be Thomas?' She giggled.

'If the cap fits, I will have to purchase you one. Thomas, do you think you could drive this?'

'Don't see why not, sir. If madam can do it, I am sure I can.'

Melissa snorted in amusement, but before carefully letting off the hand brake, she squeezed Alasdair's arm, and then they were off at a slow pace round the house.

She pulled up close to the stable block. It was a separate building from the main house – a brick-built construction in a squared-off 'U' shape with stables below and former servant accommodation above. It now had an abandoned, dilapidated air, the doors all shut up, the horses having been transferred into the smaller, more easily manageable barn that lay behind the house across a courtyard: Sheba's current home.

Henry Blake was waiting there, leaning against a closed-up stable door, having a smoke. Observing his louche ranginess, Melissa realised that anyone dismissing him as a coward would be quite wrong. He exuded an emotion that she could not quite place – something between aggression and danger. A studied sense of power, controlled but reckless. With a stab of intuition, she could feel what her wild cousin Lottie saw in him.

'Well, George has not wasted his time, has he?' Blake muttered morosely.

'True, true,' shouted Melissa over the noise of the engine. 'But she is spiffing.' She turned the motor off and hopped out, running round and opening the door for Alasdair. 'Want a spin?'

'No, I had quite enough of motor transport in France.' Then, with a glance at Melissa's crestfallen face, he added, 'But you are right, she is spiffing.'

Melissa watched Thomas unfold himself out of the rear of the little vehicle and made a mental note not to wear a dress in the back. It was only now she wondered at the practicality of their purchase. The car seemed positively tiny compared to the Brigadier's magnificent Rolls-Royce.

Henry tossed his cigarette onto the ground and crushed

it underfoot. 'We need to talk.' He nodded at Thomas. 'Alone.'

'I will find out where to house the car, Mrs Charters.' Thomas tipped his hat and made his way towards the servants' wing of the house.

'What is it?' Melissa jumped in the moment she thought Thomas was out of earshot.

'You include your wife in this?'

'In all things. Come on, let us go into the barn. My dog is in there.' Alasdair took Melissa's arm and she led the way across the yard to the old barn and to the empty stall that had been made Sheba's own. She barked in recognition. Melissa put Alasdair's hand on the stall. He opened the box and she came bounding out.

'Come on, you two.' Alasdair produced a lead from his pocket and clipped it on her collar. 'A walk, I think, before tea. Less likely to be overheard. We are meeting Maundeville at six. So it will have to be brisk.'

'You have a dog now as well?' Henry sounded amused.

'Well, she is a highly trained but failed gundog. I am wondering if she could be trained as a sort of guide dog. Alert me to pitfalls and such. I have heard they have had some success in this in Germany.' He had carefully counted the number of his footsteps into the barn and up to Sheba's stall, and he now counted them out silently as he led the way out of the barn, oblivious to Henry's surprised look and eyebrows raised at Melissa. She smiled back. Yes, Alasdair was challenging everyone's opinions about the blind today.

They walked for a few moments in silence. Melissa often noticed that Alasdair used this silence. Was it to make others uncomfortable and to encourage them to talk? Or was it his way of collecting his own thoughts? She wished she had the nerve to ask him. One day, perhaps. She turned her attention to the ground beneath their feet. It would not do if she fell and took Alasdair with her, dog or no dog. It was getting cold, and she wished she had thought to grab their mufflers and hats before they had started on this jaunt.

Henry glanced at them both, lit another gasper, then said, 'Right, so have you any clue as to what the hell is going on here?'

'Some,' stated Alasdair. 'But first tell me how you came to be here.'

'I have been seeing Lottie on and off since the war. She invited me down. Nothing odd in that.'

'Everything is odd when there have been two murders.' Alasdair came to an abrupt halt. He had been leading Melissa and now realised he hadn't a clue where they were.

Melissa, in response, took his arm more firmly and steered themselves towards a path behind the stables leading to paddocks. Henry fell in beside them.

'Fair point. Given my history, though, do you not think I am an unlikely murderer?'

'Just because you would not kill your fellow man in war does not mean you would be exempt from murder. Anyone can kill with enough motive, and, given the means and the opportunity, can be jolly successful as well.'

'Like here, you mean?'

'Hardly. We are a small group, it is clearly one of us. Adroit questioning will reveal the motive soon enough.'

'Yes, but which motive?' Henry threw out the bait, and almost as a challenge to Alasdair he smiled, bearing his teeth. Then, as if realising too late the futility of the gesture, he shrugged. He then paused and opened the gate in front of them into the paddock, then gestured to Melissa to proceed through with Alasdair. There was a faint dirt path traversing across the long grass. He shut the gate dutifully.

'What do you think? You're the reporter.' Alasdair realised he sounded agitated but this reporter was slippery as an eel.

'Cherchez la femme and all that?' Henry gave a bark of a laugh and tossed away his cigarette end. 'Well now, if I was reporting for one of the seedier papers then I would be looking for just that. Sex, scandal, infidelities. But as I do not, it is either the money or the war.'

'Anything else you have picked up?'

'There is something, but not enough for me to share. If I am to have a scoop, then I want to keep it under wraps for the moment.'

'That could be dangerous,' Alasdair warned.

'Yes, but safer all round if I do not go off half-cocked. Talking of safety, I assume you two are taking precautions.'

'Any particular reason why we should?'

'You are clearly up to your neck in whatever Maundeville is playing at, and quite clearly you are front-runners to inherit. Double jeopardy would be my headline.'

Alasdair stopped. 'Shall we turn back? Why do you think it is connected to the war?'

'What isn't these days? One half of the country wants to forget it, as they party through life thankful that they were too young or just lucky to have survived. The other half suffer as they mourn their dead or their families starve while they're looking for work.'

'I can understand your viewpoint,' muttered Alasdair. 'But how do you tie that up with what is happening here?'

'Everyone in this house is damaged in some way by the war, from the servants who lost family or had to cope with increased workloads right up to the Brigadier and his sons.'

'True, but that doesn't make murderers of them. We can hardly use the war as a motive.'

'But as a cause, as a root, an underlying infestation, an insidious clotting of the memory … that could raise a motive, surely?'

'Perhaps, but I think you were on the right lines with money or sex.'

'Alasdair, really,' protested Melissa.

'No point getting all prissy now, darling. We have a murderer in our midst.'

'Or perhaps, Henry, do you or Lottie know any of the other guests? From the war? From France?'

'What is going on with Maundeville?' Henry asked.

'Ah, that is hush, hush. I have no idea, though, whether he is here by accident, coincidence or design.'

'Oh, design I would think. I imagine it is not hard to pull the wool over the Brigadier's eyes. Lottie tells me he is a changed man since his sons died.'

'Very true. It seems to me that with your journalistic skills, you are likely to have picked up a thing or two that might help with Maundeville's investigation into the murders.'

'A ridiculous conceit,' spluttered Henry. 'He should leave it to the experts. Scotland Yard would have made short shrift of it.'

'Do you think so?' Melissa bounced in excitedly.

'Oh, without a doubt,' drawled Henry with an amused lift of one eyebrow. 'They, of course, would have arrested the butler immediately.

SEVENTEEN

Henry toddled off chuckling, already lighting another gasper, as he moved away from them. Melissa and Alasdair returned to the barn and dropped off an adoring Sheba.

Alasdair then turned to Melissa. 'You do realise he told us absolutely nothing? That he did not answer a single question, and he definitely knows or thinks he knows something?'

'Yes, but what? In a way he is right – a man who had such strong convictions about killing that he became a conscientious objector and all that entailed does seem an unlikely murderer.'

'I agree. So, let us think about motive while we walk back.'

'Well, according to you that is money or sex.'

'And spying. Money is obvious, I would have thought. Who will inherit?'

'There is also blackmail, but George is still alive.'

'Yes, but Emma, his sister, is not. Did she try her hand at blackmail?' Alasdair remembered the whispered conversation he had heard in the study last night. It could fit, but he still could not identify the voices conclusively. It was hardly likely that whoever it was would admit it. Would he ever come to terms with this sense of uselessness? How could he possibly think he could carry this off? No, leave it. He must stay focused. He mustn't let his guard down. Once he probed the soft underbelly of his soul, there was no telling what he would drag up. He had watched finer officers than himself succumb in the war. A bullet to the head or repatriated with shell shock and the whiff of madness or, even worse, cowardice.

Melissa, seemingly oblivious to his inner turmoil, continued. 'Money does not explain the death of the parlour maid, Meg, or are we just assuming she heard something or was in the wrong place at the wrong time? That German conversation Aunt Honor thought she heard could point towards your spy motive, but Emma … I just cannot see a connection.'

'We are back to the refugees, perhaps?'

'Perhaps, but we will need to talk to Bernard Lyon, and personally I think he is a nasty piece of work. Can't we leave him to Maundeville?'

'Don't forget, he phoned up the Brigadier and apparently suggested he came down this weekend specifically. His attendance this weekend is no coincidence. Well, I suppose we could let Maundeville make the running and then pick up bits of information later ourselves. He certainly seemed chummy with the Countess. That must be the reason he is down. But where he fits in with everything else, I can't imagine. Maybe it is just about money. Looking for investors?'

'Yes, well I think it all is a bloody cheek. I heard what

they said at tea. Don't you believe a word of it! If this is how people behave when you are among family, then I now understand why you have been so reluctant about emerging from the flat. I wanted to bop that Countess on the nose, and as for Bernard Lyon ... I bet most of his investments are scams!'

Alasdair looked away from her, almost as though he were scanning the horizon or trying to hide his expression. Which, of course, he was. It was so hard to be dependent on someone else. There was the issue of trust: could you rely on them not to let you fling yourself down a flight of steps or walk off the platform in front of a moving train? Then there was the privacy. He had been an intensely private person. Self-contained, happy with himself and able to think on his feet. That is what had made him such a competent soldier and spy. Absolute confidence and complete independence in the field. Of course, there had been a hiccup when he had met and married Melissa. The courtship had been short and intense, curtailed by the war. He had come back from his first leave in a state of shock. Nothing, but nothing, had prepared them for the slaughter. Staying at his parents' house in Holland Park, he found sleep escaped him, and there was a disconnect with the world around him. His mother, bless her, had decided a social whirl was what was needed and engaged him in a hectic round of parties, lunches and dinners. It was at one such that he had met the Honourable Melissa Clifford.

His father had said nothing, asked nothing, offered nothing to him, but he had, apparently, quietly talked with his circle of influence. Or so Alasdair had assumed. He never asked. His job had been to ask questions, but he never seemed capable of asking his nearest and dearest the right ones. On Alasdair's last day of leave, he had been called to Whitehall, where the first of many meetings with Sir Simon Maundeville of the Secret Intelligence Service took place. Alasdair went back to the trenches in the meantime, but more challenging missions awaited him. Missions that required his special talents. What, he wondered, were his talents now?

He cleared his throat and then said, 'So our priorities are to talk to Agnés and Bernard. Is there anyone we can eliminate? What about Arthur Baggeley?'

'I cannot see any connection. He was just too old for the war. His young wife died of the Spanish influenza. He has no children and has not remarried. I can think of no connection to France either.' He smiled; she had done her homework. What a choice he had made when he married her.

'Well, we are nearly there. Do you have to change for tea?'

'Oh, damn, I suppose I ought to. Shall we go up quickly and brush up? We should be just in time.'

They were approaching the back of the house when Alasdair halted, turned to Melissa and raised a warning finger to his lips for silence. His acute hearing had picked up the sound of raised voices from somewhere close – he assumed in the house. 'Can you hear that? Could you take us closer? It could be useful.'

'What, eavesdropping?' Honestly, darling ...'

He put his hand over her mouth and hissed in her ear. 'This is murder. Two dead and maybe more to follow. It is no time for honourable qualms. Take us closer.' They moved closer to the house, and Melissa placed his hand on the wall. From inside, they could hear quite clearly a voice raging.

'This is not ruddy happening. What am I supposed to do now? Interfering bastards! This has got to work. I won't let it fail. What more do I have to do?' It finished almost in a wail and then silence. Alasdair was about to speak when he felt warning pressure on his arm. Then there was a bang as a door slammed, followed by more silence.

'Stay there,' Melissa whispered, and he heard her light footsteps over the grass. He stood for what seemed ages but no more than a few minutes in reality. Horrified that Melissa might be about to challenge a potential murderer, he pounded the rough wall with his fingers. He did not have to wait long. He felt his fingers enclosed and stilled.

'Sorry, darling, I just could not see who it was without revealing myself outside the window. As soon as they left, I legged it as fast as I could, but I was too late, damn it. Sorry.'

'You idiot. If it was the murderer, you would have been next. Don't ever do that again.' He clutched her to him in an enveloping crush and did not let her go until his heart had ceased pounding, despite her wriggling attempts to be free. He kissed her hair and released her.

'Could you tell who it was? They sounded deranged!' she gasped.

'No!' He had to resist the urge to punch the wall. 'Was it one person or two in there, do you think?'

'No idea, but it sounded like a conversation, didn't it? The voice was deep, but I suppose it could have been a woman.'

'But you are right – they sounded mad. Not just angry, deranged, as you said. It is frustrating. It alters all the cadences of the voice. I just couldn't say. It was just like the conversation I heard in the library last night.' He stood recounting it to her, holding her hand, defying her to move.

'Yipes, Alasdair, it is four thirty. Come on, we have to change for tea!'

They rushed up the stairs and to their room, Alasdair clinging onto Melissa's arm, just above the elbow, all the while. As if by common assent, they spoke little, concentrating on the job in hand. They needed to be where everyone else was. So it was in a very short time that they descended the stairs. Melissa had thrown on a pale blue silk afternoon dress with matching shoes, some pearls and matching drop earrings. Alasdair was now in a navy blazer, flannel trousers and brogues. All had been neatly laid out ready by Thomas. 'Thank goodness that the new fashions mean I can dress myself. Having to bring a maid would be a right kerfuffle.'

'Yes, indeed, where would she fit in the car?' Alasdair teased, thankful for some light relief. He was still furious at the opportunity they had missed. He was certain that it had been the murderer. All he wanted was time to think. Whoever this person was, they were dangerous and very possibly mad. Could it be that despite all their sleuthing, it was a simple case of a person with a screw loose? How did you tell? Was he going to have to abandon reason and deduction for Melissa's psychoanalysis?

Melissa patted his hand as they reached the hallway; she had thrown caution to the wind and was not wearing gloves. She laughed. 'Well, here we go, more food.' He groaned playfully, happy that she sounded as though she had regained her usual good mood.

They entered the drawing room, and Melissa could see that all the low tables were loaded with delicacies; she panicked as to how Alasdair would cope. Once again, though, Smithers had had forethought, and he motioned to two dining chairs either side of a small mahogany half-moon table set against one wall. 'Perfect, Smithers.' Melissa beamed at him. 'How thoughtful you are.'

'Not at all, my lady. Her Ladyship has just poured. Tea for two?'

'Yes please.'

'How many ladies can you fit in one room?' muttered Alasdair. 'He's laying it on a bit thick, isn't he? Who else is here?'

'Aunt Honor, obviously. Not Uncle Reggie, he is hardly the tea sort. I don't see George or Henry Blake either. Perhaps you could have ducked out of this and had a rest.'

'We are meant to be working, remember?'

'True. Ah, here is Bernard Lyon. I thought he wouldn't miss tea, the size of him. If the Brigadier reminds me of a benevolent walrus with those moustaches, Bernard Lyon would be a bloated seal.' Alasdair choked momentarily and she grinned at his astonished face. She continued. 'Agnés Baume. The vicar, again. Is he moving in? Can we discount him?'

'Depends where he was during the war. I cannot think he has anything else to gain. What the hell is that?'

'The Countess has made her entrance, very fetching in a green silk, tasselled number. Once again, more jazz club than afternoon tea.'

'Do I detect snobbery?'

'Perhaps, but she isn't wearing gloves either.' Melissa grinned.

'Perhaps this is your opportunity to compare fashion tips.'

'I think not, she is best left to Maundeville. I cannot see us being bosom friends, can you? Oh hello, Vicar, coming to join us?' Melissa had watched him approach carrying a plate of dainties. He now set them on the table, looked around and then carried over a chair to join them, thus blocking her view of the rest of the party. 'How kind,' she muttered.

'Thought it was the least I could do.' He reached over, tapped Alasdair's arm and then clasped his hand in a formal handshake. 'Harold James, the local vicar at St John's. I am sorry, but I was a little out of my depth last night. It was kind of your aunt to invite me, but it was a bit daunting.'

Melissa found herself warming towards him. 'Yes, well. I suppose it is at first, but I am sure you will soon get the hang of it all. Have you been here long?'

'Only about three months.'

'Oh, where were you before that?'

'Just a lowly curate in an inner London parish. I am sure you would not know it.'

'What about during the war? Alasdair told me the chaplains were absolutely marvellous.'

If he picked up her tone, he ignored her. 'Yes indeed, I was a chaplain in the army. I did two years at the front in the end. Recruited in 1916. My first posting was the Somme. You can imagine that it was definitely a baptism of fire. I sometimes wondered how I survived at all. Over one hundred and fifty chaplains died during the war, you know. That is why we were awarded royal status.'

Melissa turned to him in surprise. 'But what did you do? Did you fight?'

'Oh no, no. We were unarmed, mostly left to our own devices, I was lucky our Colonel just let me get on with it. Sometimes I went to the front, helped the wounded, prayed, gave last rights, conducted burials, that sort of thing. When it got too much I went to the hospitals and tried to give succour to the wounded.'

'Yes, a chaplain sat with me when I was at the field station, Padre.' Alasdair said. . I wonder where he is now.'

'Would you recognise him?' The vicar's voice deepened in empathy.

'Yes, I will remember his voice to the end of my days. I would like to thank him.'

Tears welled in Melissa's eyes. She'd had no idea. None whatsoever. Would Alasdair ever confide in her? What was he afraid of? That she would love him less? How was that even possible? 'Do you recognise anyone here?' she asked the vicar quietly. 'So many here seem to have been involved in the war.'

'No, of course, not.' The vicar recoiled, shocked, and stood up, having to catch the back of the chair to stop it falling. Surprised at his reaction, Melissa moved back instinctively, suddenly seeing the man behind the mild façade.

'I'm sorry, Mrs Charters, my nerves are all to pieces. This murder brings it all back. France was a large theatre of war. Unusual it certainly would be to meet anyone from that time, I can assure you. However, it is the flock in the here and now I must attend to.' He turned and began walking away.

'But coincidences do happen, do they not?' muttered Alasdair quietly.

EIGHTEEN

Melissa looked around and was surprised to see the vicar make his way over to Bernard Lyon. It seemed such an unusual pairing that she paused and observed them. A brief exchange took place. The vicar flushed red and moved away quickly, skirting the Countess, who looked bemused to be snubbed by a man, and he joined Rose and Lottie, who were seated at a small table at the far end of the room. Bernard Lyon looked pleased with himself – the cat that got the cream, Melissa thought.

Her attention was then attracted by Agnés Beaume. Agnés appeared both distracted and agitated at the same time. She approached the Countess and handed her a packet of cigarettes. 'No, no, you fool. I needed the case. The gold case. I do not smoke cigarettes out of a packet. What are you thinking, you stupid girl?'

'Madame, I could not find the case. I have looked everywhere. Are you sure it is not …'

'This is incroyable. You are an imbecile. If you have lost it, that is at least half a year's wages.' The Countess had made no attempt to lower her voice; if anything, it took on an increased depth.

'Madame.' Agnés voice wobbled. Tears welled, but then she visibly took a deep breath. 'I think not, Madame la Comtesse.' Her voice sharpened. 'Otherwise I might wish to tell what I know.' She seemed oblivious to the audience's rapt attention around them.

An odd look passed over the face of the Countess. 'Poof, what do you know?' She shrugged in an exaggerated Gallic gesture. 'No matter. I am sure the case will turn up. No doubt you have just mislaid it.' She turned away and made quite an exhibition of lighting a cigarette in a carved-bone cigarette holder which she had removed from her beaded clutch bag.

Agnés flushed and then, as if only now realising she was the centre of attention, looked around like a frightened child, caught out doing something wrong.

Melissa raised her hand and beckoned to the vacant seat between them. Agnés appeared to prevaricate only for a moment. Clearly having sat next to Alasdair the night before had convinced her they were harmless. With a quick smile of relief, Agnés made her way over to them and sat at their table.

'Hello, Agnés, let us see if Smithers can rustle you up a cup of tea. Oh, look, there he is.' Melissa realised she was gabbling but wanted to cover up the poor girl's embarrassment and at the same time indicate who had now joined them to Alasdair.

As usual, he seemed ahead of the game as he turned slightly towards Agnés and said quietly, 'What an awful woman. How do you put up with her?'

'The war made paupers of so many of us. I fled from Belgium to relations in France. I met the Countess through them. It seemed prudent at the time to accept her employment.'

'Gosh, you speak superb English, much better than my useless French. Almost without an accent,' Melissa exclaimed.

'I speak German too, but not as well.'

'Oh, then it is Alasdair you should talk to – it is he who is the expert in languages in this marriage.'

'But your English is so good, I would not need my languages for you. Was it your skill in languages that recommended you to the Countess?' he said smoothly.

'No, I think it was that I was cheap,' she muttered drily. 'That and it clearly amused her to employ' – she lowered her voice further – 'a real aristocrat as a companion – though servant might be more accurate.' Melissa raised her eyebrows. 'Mais oui,' she responded. 'It pains me to tell you that my grandfather was a vicomte in Belgium. The Countess is only a countess by marriage.'

'Oh, she is married. Where is her husband?' Melissa glanced theatrically around the room.

'She says he was lost in the war – but who knows? She is such a liar.'

'Really?' Melissa leant forward, inviting confidence, but Agnés appeared to have taken fright again. She returned her cup to the saucer with a sharp click.

'Well, I must go. I am sure her cigarette case is in her bag. No doubt she will find it later. You have been very kind. À bientôt.' She inclined her head, gave a small smile and left the room.

'Well, that was interesting,' Melissa enthused.

'Indeed. I would love to know more about the origins of La Comtesse, wouldn't you?'

'Well, maybe Maundeville can fill us in. It must be

almost time for our meeting.' Melissa checked her wristlet watch. 'Gosh, so it is. Come on let us go now.'

They made their way rather more sedately this time towards the large library. Aware that she had bounced Alasdair off walls in her hurry previously, Melissa walked more slowly and carefully. In an old house like this, founded in such graceful times from the last century, the hallways were thankfully large and easily able to accommodate two people abreast. As they passed a door in the hallway close to the more imposing double doors of the large library, she stopped, opened the door and peeped in, trying to refresh her memory of the house. She had missed this room yesterday. It was suddenly as she remembered it: a small compact library room connected to the bigger library by an internal door. She tried to remember. Was the other side of the door fake shelves and books? She thought it was. The opposite wall was covered in enclosed book cases with glass fronts. Perhaps this was where the valuable books were kept? Once again on the opposite wall there was a fireplace, the grate made up but not lit. Despite this, the room, she felt, had a cosy, relaxed feel that she loved. There was none of the musty smell that accompanied the larger library next door.

'What are you doing now?' Alasdair sounded irritable.

'Oh, sorry, darling, I got distracted. This is a lovely room next to the large library. I guess you could call it the little library?' She attempted a joke. His lips curled but he made no comment. She closed the door quietly and they moved on down the corridor.

A short while later, they were seated before Maundeville. He was alone, the remains of his afternoon tea still on the desk before him. He appeared weary and confirmed it with his words. 'Let us make this quick. I am getting old. I need a quick shut-eye or I will never make dinner. I don't know how the police put up with it. The amount of dross and obfuscation I have heard today has been well-nigh impossible to sift, and Godfrey is no help.'

'Have you interviewed everyone now?'

'All except that damn banker. Slippery as an eel…keeps going missing when Godfrey goes to find him.' He raised a placating hand. 'But do not worry – I will catch up with him at some point, no doubt, but frankly I cannot see what use he might be.'

'He is in thick with the Countess and he knew the first victim,' Alasdair said.

'Did he, by jove? But I hardly think merchant bankers go around murdering people.'

'Huh,' muttered Alasdair. 'My father is a barrister and you should hear him on the subject of the banking fraternity.'

'Ah, yes, I forgot your father is Sir Hector Charters, isn't he? He helped out one of the princes, did he not? One of their little problems.' His voice was dry.

'Yes, indeed.' Alasdair had no intention of being drawn or diverted by his father's illustrious career. 'But back to today. Do you have any forensic evidence at all? What would Spilsbury make of all this, do you think?'

'Nothing. I doubt even he could help. Although it may come to it. The bodies are packed with ice, just in case,' Maundeville replied gloomily. He glanced up and grimaced as he appeared to notice Melissa turning pale and shivering at his words. He stood up, went over to the fire and, brandishing the poker with intent, savagely jabbed at the logs.

Turning, he returned to his seat, cleared his throat, and said, 'Well you did ask. There is no getting away from this if you want to be part of the investigation.' But he continued, softening his voice as if that could soften the horror of the information. 'Both were stabbed through the heart. Death would have been pretty quick. The knives were from a set kept in the butler's pantry. It was not kept locked. Appalling household management. It is a wonder there is any silver left. They are sharp carving knives with solid silver handles. Wiped clean so no chance of any fingerprints even if we were equipped to take them. Similar MO in the killing – both stabbed in the back, through the ribcage and into the heart. Could have been a man or a woman, according to the doctor – the knives are that sharp. Like slicing butter, apparently.'

'But some knowledge or expertise must be shown in that they clearly missed the ribs?' commented Alasdair.

'Yes, true. Bayonet practice, eh? But it could conceivably be luck. However, the most important point is that there is still one knife missing from the set. Servants insist it was a full set before this weekend. So …'

'The murderer may not yet be finished.' Alasdair completed the sentence.

NINETEEN

'Good Lord, this is terrible. Do we really have to sit around and wait to be picked off next? Oh dear, now I sound like Bernard Lyon.' Melissa covered her mouth with her hand; this had ceased to be fun. Exciting, yes, but who on earth could it be? She felt like she was in a stinking fug. 'But are we any nearer to solving this? Is there anything we can do?'

'Not that I can see,' muttered Alasdair morosely. 'Wait a minute, though. What about constructing a timeline for the murder and plot where people were?'

'We need more information,' snapped Maundeville. 'And fast.'

'So what about some sort of visual stimulus? You might find it helpful.'

'I know what you need,' exclaimed Melissa. 'It's a blackboard and chalk. I bet there is still one from the nursery. I'll get Smithers to have a look and fetch it down.'

'Not sure I see the point,' Maundeville muttered. 'But go ahead. There is at least room in here to set it up.'

Melissa leapt up, rang the bell and a whispered conversation ensued at the door.

'Please tell us more about the Countess before you retire for your rest,' Alasdair said.

'Well, we have been tracking her for some time. She came to our notice in 1915, flitting between Paris and London. Her credentials seemed impeccable. Too impeccable, if you know what I mean. As far as we can ascertain, she really is a countess by marriage to Count Henri de Orleon. His whereabouts, however, remain a mystery. There is a crumbling chateau in Alsace but no sign of Le Comte.'

'Hmm, remarkably near to the German border.'

'Yes, but she is clever – declares she hates the place, and we have been unable to pinpoint her spending any time there, despite exhaustive research though the travel records that are available. If she did, she went either under an assumed name that we don't know, or she used some untraceable form of transport.'

'Shame.'

'But what makes you so sure that she is a spy?' Confusion resonated in Melissa's voice as she resumed her seat. What was he not telling them? If he kept things back, he who had recruited them in the first place, what would be their chances of success? And had they been set up to fail? What was the American word? Were they being made into patsies?

'There have been too many coincidences when she has been around. Information getting into the wrong hands, loose-lipped officers allowing her to tip off the Germans, but we have not been able to source how she has done it. If you remember yourself, Alasdair, she was one of our persons of interest later in the war.'

'Yes, but I have a nagging feeling that there is something

wrong or not right about her…something in her voice. I just cannot isolate it at the moment. I need to hear her talk more, but there is fat chance of that as she thinks I am an imbecile.' Alasdair mimicked her voice.

'Yes, but it could mean that she drops her guard when you are around. You will just have to try and keep near to her. That is the best advice I can give you.'

There was a knock at the door and Smithers entered with a young lad carrying a large blackboard and easel, and he had even found chalk. Melissa leapt forward. 'You really are a star, Smithers.'

'Leave it now. I really must retire or I will fall asleep during the fish course.' Maundeville really was irritable.

Melissa took that as their cue to leave. She led Alasdair carefully back to their rooms, guided him to an easy chair with his back to the window and flopped onto the bed. 'Well, what are we meant to make of all this now? It is so frustrating.'

Glancing across at Alasdair, she was worried; there were dark circles under his eyes and his skin seemed stretched too tightly over his face. The strain was beginning to show.

'Do you have your notebook? Can we go through what we have gleaned so far?' he said.

'Who are our main suspects?' Now this was more like it: real sleuthing. She went over to her bag and collected it, opened the book and pulled out the propelling pencil at the ready.

'Forget suspects,' he said. 'What do we know about each person staying here? Let's create a profile of each one and see if that gets us anywhere. Can we assume that the servants are above suspicion? Thomas said they all appeared honestly shocked, frightened and confused. They were all fond of Meg. Apparently she was a bright little thing. Quick on the uptake.'

'Too quick on the uptake, you think? Was that why she was murdered? I would have thought the other servants can be discounted. Unless, of course, she confided in anyone. You are right. I will talk to Smithers. There are not any obviously new servants that I have seen. There just seems to be a steady dwindling of those I have known over the years around us. Meg would have been hard-pressed to find a confidant among them.'

'Dwindling now even more with poor Meg.'

'Yes, that is particularly bloody, poor little thing.' Guilt slipped in and took hold in Melissa's rib cage. She wrapped her arms around her body, as if hugging herself would make it better.

'Well, we have to remember that Meg was a victim but why? She mentioned Germany or Germans. Was it just that she was in the wrong place at the wrong time and heard something she was not meant to? Can we surmise what she is likely to have heard? Was she killed because the murderer knew she had heard something that put them in danger? What was it? Did she see them going into the butler's pantry? Emerging with a box of knives? Or overheard Emma talking?'

'That is what has been puzzling me: how did the killer know she heard something?'

'Well, they saw her downstairs, of course. The screaming… I hadn't thought about it before. It must have been her. So maybe she was killed just in case?'

'That sounds awfully cold-blooded. Even for a murderer.'

'Yes, but worse still, I just had a thought,' Alasdair said. 'Could anyone have overheard Honor telling you about what Meg had told her?'

'I am not sure. I shut her up pretty quick, but I suppose it is possible.'

'Damn, there is nothing definite. How about the other servants?'

'Davies is new, although as estate manager he is hardly a servant.'

'But he works and lives on the estate. No one mentions seeing him in the house, though, do they?'

'No, true, but we must check just to rule him out. As an army veteran, he would be a practised killer.'

'What, like you?' Melissa retorted, but on a look from Alasdair she added, 'Agreed, I'll note it. Shall we move on to family?'

'If you think so. I am not sure they are relevant either now.' He sounded morose.

'True but perhaps we can eliminate some? What do you think?'

Alasdair nodded.

'Lottie? The Honourable Charlotte Dauncey, perhaps I should properly call her. She has a connection to France as she drove an ambulance during the latter part of the war, but I can see no reason why she should be a spy or why she should murder Emma. We all spent holidays together as children and kept in touch since. Perhaps not as often as we ought, but enough to still be close.' That pain again. Why did guilt hurt so?

'Many murders are domestic affairs, do not forget.'

'Granted, but what about…what did you say we had

to look for?' She counted them off on her fingers. 'Motive, means and opportunity. So, motive, can you think of any?'

'Money?'

'But she might inherit anyway – she does not need to bump off Emma.'

'Well she might. Incidentally, I have not told you Brigadier Ferguson's news. He is loaded.'

'Loaded? With what?' Melissa asked, sitting up in surprise.

'Money. He apparently invested with Bernard Lyon during the war and made a packet. Feels guilty as hell now, but at the time just wanted to hand things over to someone to manage, and it sounds as if he did rather well.'

'Hmm. Now if you had said Bernard Lyon had lost him a packet, I would not have been surprised.'

'Yes,' Alasdair said, 'that may be his motive for being here this weekend – to gain back some of Brigadier Ferguson's dosh. But don't forget – we may be the only ones, other than Bernard Lyon, of course, that know the Brigadier is cash rich now. Keep schtum until we get the go-ahead from Brigadier Ferguson. I doubt even Maundeville knows.'

'Oh dear, this is hard.' Melissa sighed. 'You are right – looking at the house at the moment, it is in dire need of an overhaul. They have updated some things and not others. It looks like Aunt and Uncle started on modernisation and then gave up. Certainly, judging by appearances, you might think there is not enough money to go around. So Lottie could have a motive at a pinch. I'll grant that. What about opportunity?'

'We were all in bed, allegedly. Did you see her on the landing when you heard the crash?'

'Sorry, no, I can't remember.'

'When I was with Maundeville, Godfrey remembered seeing Henry Blake, so he can't provide her with an alibi.'

'Oh, Alasdair, you beast, of course he can't! Oh, but then she also could have the opportunity if she has no alibi?'

'Means. Presumably we all have access to the unlocked butler's pantry for the knife. If she drove an ambulance, she could have picked up basic anatomy. Enough to know where to stick the knife in most successfully.'

'Oh, Alasdair, that is horrible.' Melissa shivered. 'No, I just can't see that as something she would do. She went to France to save lives and was jolly brave. I really cannot imagine her murdering someone. One must have to include psychology in the calculations as well, surely. Think of that brilliant Agatha Christie I read you last year.'

'Ah yes, Poirot and his "little grey cells" – is that what you are alluding to?'

'Yes, exactly, and Carl Jung.'

'Oh, spare me your new-fangled psychoanalysis phase, please.'

'But…' Melissa began. She still had high hopes that it could help Alasdair cope with his blindness, if only he would listen. If only he would talk to someone. He was so prickly about anything that might be termed emotional. Stiff upper lip all the way and, she acknowledged shrewdly, suffering because of it. It was so painful watching someone you loved struggle in pain. The night sweats, the nightmares. He refused to talk about them; it was his own private battleground onto which she was not invited. She had learnt, to her cost, not to venture there. He would not, so far, be moved.

'No one knows what is in someone else's head and what they are capable of. That is what I learnt from the war. We need facts not wild suppositions,' he replied.

'All right, so Lottie is still a suspect.' She sounded sulky even to her own ears, but sometimes he was so impossible.

'Let us see if anyone saw her on the landing coming out of her room. Then we can reconsider.'

'Henry Blake?' Her attempt at sarcasm fell flat.

'Stick to family, for now. What about George?'

'OK. George Ferguson, brother of the first victim, Emma. Motive? Well, we have none. He was cross Emma was killed, remember, as he hoped to blackmail Bernard Lyon. Of course, if he is capable of blackmail and wants the money for his business… but no, killing Emma is not going to give him much more, is it? He is hardly going to kill his sister for her share, is he?'

'I think you are right. Now if he had been murdered, I could understand it! This just doesn't make sense. There is something, though – both Godfrey and Henry Blake mentioned George making an untoward comment over the port. Perhaps that will give us a clue. How can we find out?'

Alasdair turned towards his wife and then they both said, 'Smithers.'

TWENTY

'OK,' Alasdair said. 'Let us start making a list of things to do at the back of your book. Otherwise we will forget. I used to make meticulous notes.' That pain. Like a punch to the gut. Move on, move on, he thought. Use the past. Don't wallow.

'Yes, and I bet they were in code,' muttered Melissa. It would take a while for her to readjust her thinking and forgive his subterfuge. She was his wife, for heaven's sake. How could he have kept her in the dark about his being a former spy? Blow the Official Secrets Act! 'Fire away.'

'Check up on staff. Find out what the hell was said over the port. Create a list of suspects. For a start, the Countess, Cousin Lottie, George…put a question mark. I think he looks in the clear, but you never can be sure. What about the Honourable Rose?' He felt more on an even keel now.

'I cannot see a single reason. What would be her motive? All she wants is a husband. Granted, she may be a bit obsessive about it, but going around murdering people is not a normal form of courtship, is it?' Melissa's reply had a snap in it.

'Fair enough,' he said. 'Put her in another column.

Now, Henry Blake?'

'I thought we had discounted him as he was a conscientious objector. Also, surely he reports on crime, not commits it.' Her voice had softened. He was, as always, forgiven.

Alasdair chuckled. 'You are loving this, aren't you?'

'Well, yes and no. Sleuthing like this with you is fun, but the murders have been beastly, and, to be frank, underneath it all I am feeling, well, fear and excitement and all overlaid with the collywobbles.'

'That is just the feeling I had before going over the top in the trenches during the war or on an undercover mission. I think it shows that you have a strong streak of bravery, level-headedness and, most importantly, a real sense of self-preservation. Which, to be honest, we are going to need to come out of this unscathed.' He missed the look of delighted astonishment that came over her face at his words, but not the emotional throat-clearing.

'I assume we can put Aunt and Uncle in the potentially innocent column?'

'Yes, I cannot see a motive.' Alasdair was silent for a moment or two. 'Unless, of course, they know something about their sons' deaths that is untoward. That might tip them over the edge.'

'Hardly likely, though, is it? But we could get Maundeville to probe about at the Army Board in Whitehall.' She paused. 'What about Bernard Lyon? All that stuff about being run off the road? Is he a murderer or a target?'

'Could be both. Bernard Lyon is not stupid, Mellie,

you should not make that mistake with him. A banker of his standing does not get there by charm.'

'Yes, well, I think we need to investigate him too. He is definitely fishy, even if he is an eminent banker. Hang on, wait a minute – why has Uncle Reggie got him down to help with the will? Why not a lawyer? Or why doesn't uncle just hand out some advances now? Might be a bit safer... less chance of anyone else getting bumped off. That would then remove the money motive in one fell swoop.'

'Yes, I might suggest that to him, but later. We need to smoke the murderer out somehow.'

'Oh gawd, look at the time! They will be ringing the first gong soon.' Melissa shut the book with a snap, not quite so keen on that suggestion.

'Do not leave that lying around, will you? Best keep it in your evening bag. Also, did you bring your little pea-shooter with you?'

'Well, now you mention it, I did.' When she saw the incredulous expression on his face, she quickly added, 'Only because I thought I might have a chance for a quick potshot somewhere. Uncle used to set up a target in one of the barns years ago. I don't want to get out of practice.' How could she explain to him the longing for excitement, action of any kind. Even murder beat endless lone games of patience – in spades.

'Is it loaded? If not, load it and keep that in your evening bag as well. We cannot be too careful. You are right to feel the collywobbles. There is danger here.'

There was a knock at the door. Melissa leapt up, more in fright than enthusiasm. She really needed to get a grip, she thought, as she cautiously opened the door. It was Thomas, the valet. 'Madam, I have drawn a bath. Would you like to take it while I put out sir's evening clothes?'

Melissa smiled. He was so discreet; with no dressing room here, it made dressing for dinner a bit of a dance. 'Thank you, we will be OK after that, Oh, no, wait. Show me again how to tie a perfect white tie.'

As Melissa made her way back from the bathroom, one of two bathrooms shared by the five bedrooms on that wing, she appraised the layout. She acknowledged that she was day-dreaming about what might not come to pass but was also astute enough to know that this was something she wanted. These five bedrooms and two bathrooms, linen cupboard and two lavatories, would, with work, make a very roomy and comfortable apartment. She presumed the other wing was similar. They could make that work. How often, really, were the Fergusons likely to have hordes of guests? Or perhaps they could convert the ground floor and some of the guest wing on the second floor into a maisonette? She sighed, realising that she was getting ahead of herself. The question should be: did Alasdair want this, and if he did, could he ever find his way around this enormous house on his own?

An hour later they were ready, just as the second gong sounded. Melissa had, this evening, picked a shocking pink drop-waisted silk dress. From the hips to the below knee, the hem was encrusted with sequins which gave the hem weight and let the dress sashay as she swung her hips. The neck was decorous, in contrast to the tiny spaghetti straps, a boat-neck and drop sleeves, daringly leaving her shoulders bare. She fixed a matching pink-sequined band in her hair and grinned, satisfied with how she looked in the mirror. Not that she was competitive, she assured herself, but she wanted to give the Countess a run for her money this evening.

Alasdair was once again in formal evening clothes, this time with a tie perfect to his satisfaction. Was it only last night that they had gone down to dinner in such trepidation, little thinking that all their social fears would be overtaken by murder? She turned, put her arms around Alasdair's neck and kissed him. 'Come on, let us brave the cocktails and see what happens tonight. We still haven't finished our list. Is Arthur Baggeley out of the picture? And what about the vicar?'

'Baggeley, yes, I think so. But there is something odd about that vicar. I can't quite put my finger on it yet. It is sitting at the back of my brain, but I'll get there.'

TWENTY-ONE

SATURDAY EVENING

Cocktails were again available in the blue drawing room. Melissa pondered once more on the presence of ice. Did Aunt Honor have one of those new American-style refrigerators? Usually it was only the swankiest hotels in town that had ice for drinks. Modern in some things and dismally Victorian in others. It was clear that they needed help, but were her and Alasdair the right people for the job?

She handed Alasdair a Martini in a whisky glass and took herself a small Pimms in a long crystal glass, praying that it was not too strong. As luck would have it, Smithers had taken Alasdair's arm and had led him slightly away. This gave her some time for reflection. She looked around, as they had been some of the last to come in. The room looked full. Full of glamorous people in full evening dress taking their fill. She wondered how much longer this style of weekend could continue. If Alasdair was correct and Uncle Reggie did have money, that might explain it, but how many other people could afford to put up fifteen or so guests for three nights, all meals and drinks included? When she thought about the reports in the newspapers of the starving workers in northern England or saw the ex-servicemen begging on the roads, she despaired. Perhaps whoever was doing the killing was just culling a class that now had no useful purpose?

Her musings were interrupted when she noticed Smithers abruptly leave Alasdair's side and move away, apparently to talk to Henry, who had also arrived late to cocktails.

She quickly went to the rescue, and, approaching Alasdair, stroked his arm to let him know that she was there. He always seemed to recognise her; she still hadn't a clue how. ''Tis I. Are you OK?'

'Interesting. Can't talk now. Most peculiar. Smithers' reaction was bizarre.'

'Well, it looks like tonight is a repeat of last night. The vicar is here, as is Arthur Baggeley. Oh, I have an idea there. Just a minute – I must talk to Aunt Honor.' She slipped across the room, took Aunt Honor's arm and whispered in her ear. Aunt Honor looked startled at her request for a moment but then smiled, nodded and left the room. Smiling to herself, Melissa returned to Alasdair's side. She squeezed his arm.

'Well what are you so pleased about?'

'What do you mean?' Melissa was amazed; it was almost as though he could see her smirk.

'You always squeeze my arm with a certain intensity when you are excited. This time it was not the most intense, so you are not afraid or very excited. This is mild excitement. Ergo, pleasure.'

Melissa reached up and kissed his cheek. 'You really are a wonder, you know.' Two bright spots of colour appeared high on Alasdair's cheeks, and Melissa was able to see his pleasure now. 'And how do you know it is me?' She decided to risk being personal. This weekend was proving to be one of revelations, especially in their marriage.

'Your smell,' he replied. As if it was obvious.

'But I must use the same perfume as countless other women.'

'Yes, perhaps, but everyone has their own unique smell. Perfume smells differently on other people. I must admit, I have not conducted copious research into the unique smell of women.' He grinned. 'I suppose I could, just for research purposes?'

'Oh, you beast,' exclaimed Melissa. This, she turned into a cough at the last minute as they were being approached by Arthur Baggeley. 'How are you, Arthur?'

'Very well, very well, thank you, Melissa. How are you finding things…' His voice trailed off. 'Sorry, a bit tactless. It is so hard to know how to behave. Murder is not the norm, is it?'

'I do not think anything is the norm this weekend. I was just thinking how many other estates can still put on a weekend like this?'

'Well, of course, Reginald did well with his stocks and shares. As, to be honest, did I. We both invested with Bernard over there.' He lowered his voice, 'Ghastly man, but a sound financier.'

'Up until now,' Alasdair commented.

Arthur glared at him. 'What do you mean, Alasdair? What have you heard?'

'Nothing, Arthur, other than, as I told Reginald, with little else to do since the war I have taken a keen interest in the stock market. Melissa reads me the Financial Times, and I just think it all sounds a bit volatile at the moment.'

'Hmm, but a faint heart never won etc., etc.'

'True.' Alasdair's response was cool. 'I guess it depends if you can afford to lose. Have you known Bernard for long?'

If Arthur noticed the abrupt change in topic, he was far too well-mannered to comment. He crinkled his eyes for a moment while he appeared to think. His large grey eyes rested on Alasdair's face, as if daring him to see. It gave Melissa a moment to consider him. He had sandy hair with odd flecks of grey, a bit like a rough-coated collie. He was not too tall, nor overweight, and she thought not too old, perhaps about fifty. She had to firmly resist a giggle when it struck her that she was eyeing him up like a piece of horseflesh. Which was really just what she was doing: marriageable horseflesh. Yes, she thought, he will do very nicely. We all just need to live long enough.

Realising that, in her reverie, she had missed part of the conversation, she tuned back to it. 'As I said, it was all down to Reginald,' Arthur was saying.

'Forgive me for saying, Arthur, but as you can see, my eyes are not what they were. Were you in the war?' Alasdair probed further. He was sadly unable to see the crimson tide of embarrassment that crept from Arthur's winged collar upwards.

'No, I was considered too old at the start of the war and was also in a reserved occupation with the estate. I tried to enlist later when it was clear that the bloom of our youth were being slaughtered. How could I look Reginald in the eye? First Henry, then Richard the following year. Anyway, failed the medical, weak chest apparently. Course

I was approaching forty by then, and with no military experience…ridiculous exercise, and then it was Harriet who died from that damn Spanish Flu. And not just her, our unborn child. I often wondered if it was retribution for not trying harder.'

'Oh, you cannot think that,' Melissa intervened. 'In her condition, she may have been weakened. Surely no one holds the war against you.'

'No, but I do.' He blinked and gave a sad smile, suddenly looking very vulnerable and not a little surprised at what he had revealed to this empathic couple.

As Arthur moved off, his hands clasped behind his back, one hand tapping the other, Melissa lightly touched Alasdair's arm to warn him and he stood still as she quickly caught Arthur up. 'Sorry, Arthur, just one more thing. What happened, or was said, over the port when Alasdair left with Sir Maundeville? Everyone seems to be a little odd about it.'

'Not surprised. Terrible sewer comment from your cousin George. Still, Reginald sorted him out. I have no idea what he was up to. You could talk to George, but I do not advise it.' He turned on his heel and walked brusquely away towards the melee forming near the door.

Confused now, Melissa returned to Alasdair, cogitating on what she had heard. He may be a little older than me, Melissa conceded to herself, but he could be just right for Rose. She had said herself that she was desperate, or was that her mother? Unless one or both of them is a murderer? She shuddered. Someone was walking over her grave.

TWENTY-TWO

Within minutes, the last gong sounded and they processed into dinner on this, the second night of their stay. This time, Melissa noticed that Reginald had the pleasure of the Countess's arm. Tonight, she was in a skin-tight black fishtail dress with a very risqué low back. A beautiful creation, but Melissa was pleased to note that the stark black seemed to leech the colour from the Countess's face in spite of the splash of scarlet lipstick, making her seem older, feral, or perhaps her real age? It was a hard, calculating image, an image that brooked no mercy. Melissa then gave up a silent prayer that the table layout would be kind to them again this evening.

She was surprised and somewhat appalled when she realised that she was seated next to Reginald, seated as custom demanded at the head of the table, with Alasdair beside her. They were in pole position and very exposed. Beyond Alasdair was Rose with Arthur beside her. So her matchmaking at table had been successful, but why had she and Alasdair been seated here? Was this another of the Brigadier's tests? She looked across the table into the eyes of the Countess de Orleon seated opposite; her eyes glittered with malice, or was it amusement? She made Melissa's skin crawl. It was almost as if she could read her mind. A slow insolent smile crept over her face. Malice it was, then.

Next to the Countess was Bernard Lyon, another person that normally Melissa would have actively avoided. Beside him, thank goodness, was Lottie – at least one friendly face within reach. She glanced further down that side of the table; diagonally opposite her, at the far end next to Lady Honor, was Maundeville. He gave her what appeared to be a genuine smile and an almost imperceptible wink. So that was how it was to be.

She touched Alasdair's arm and explained the configuration of the table to him. She then glanced down at the table setting. Horror of horrors – the first course appeared to be soup. Soup was one of the more difficult foods to for a blind person to manage, especially in a formal setting. Hell, even for a sighted person it could be a nightmare. The accidental slurp. The capacity for dribbling it down the front of you or over the pristine white starched tablecloth. She sighed and muttered, 'Soup first.'

The Brigadier interrupted the hushed conversation around the table by clearing his throat and asking the Reverend Harold James to say grace. He had a warm, melodious voice and was clearly not as nervous as the night before. The grace was formal but simple and lent a calm dignity to the meal and to the vicar. He might just do, Melissa thought.

Smithers collected a tureen from the dumb waiter and began ladling out the soup into the wide gold-rimmed bone china soup bowls. It looked like vichyssoise. Just as he was serving Melissa, then Alasdair in his turn, the Countess made her first move. 'I am reliably informed that you are an 'onerable. What does that mean? We do not have such distinctions in France.'

'My grandfather is an earl, Baron Clifford,' Melissa replied. 'My father is Lady Honor's brother, Lord Clifford, and as his daughter I am entitled to the honorific the Honourable. Terribly confusing, what?' She added a drawl for effect.

'And your husband, is he also aristocratic? Despite his affliction.'

Melissa almost slurped her own soup. 'I am sure Alasdair would be more than happy to fill you in, but as you asked, he is the son of Sir Hector Charters, a baronet.'

'Not the famous, or should I say infamous, barrister extraordinaire?' interrupted Bernard. 'He sorts out all the upper echelons of society when they get into trouble, doesn't he? I heard he even helped out the odd royal. Useful man to know.' He glanced an aside to the Countess and leered unpleasantly.

An in-joke, Melissa surmised. She glanced at Alasdair; he was steadily consuming his soup. Anxious to deflect the Countess, she enquired, 'And your own title, Countess? Were you always a countess?'

Bernard spluttered in response and the Countess's lips thinned. 'No, I married a count.' Melissa opened her mouth to enquire further, but her Uncle Reginald, Brigadier Ferguson, was first.

'Yes, but just a Froggie count, ten a penny of them in France, I don't doubt. Still, we won't hold it against you, will we, Melissa?' He guffawed loudly. 'Where is he anyway?'

Melissa lowered her eyes to the soup, not wanting to appear too interested in the answer. Remember, fluffy aristo, she repeated in her head like a mantra.

'I am completely désolé. He is missing.' The Countess shrugged.

'Oh, how simply ghastly,' Melissa replied. 'So many men did not come back from the war, so many lost, unheard from again. Was he at the front?'

'No, no, he was far too old. He went out riding one day and simply, what can I say? Disparu.'

'What, horse and all?' Alasdair had finished his soup.

'It is, as you English say, an enigma. No horse, no rider, it was poof.' She gave an exaggerated Gallic shrug of her shoulders and waved one hand. 'Like he disappeared in, what is your expression, smoke?'

'But can anyone just disappear in war? Was your estate near the fighting?'

The Countess glared at Alasdair, then, perhaps realising he could not see her, she changed her tone. 'I find this all too distressing. Please, we will speak no more of it.' She turned to Bernard and, clearly as a distraction, asked him a question in a low voice.

Effectively cut off from discourse to his right, Brigadier Ferguson turned to Melissa. 'So good to be back, what? Had a good dekko around? Think you could stand it? What do you think?'

Melissa glanced down the table; the one thing her uncle was not was discreet.

Lottie was sitting between Bernard and Henry Blake, and she grinned. 'Yes, do tell, Melissa. Have you decided yet? Are you really going to take this on?'

'Well, that is rather presumptuous. Uncle invited us all down,' she muttered lamely.

'Oh, don't be a chump, Mellie. George is up to his eyes in motors, and I loathe the countryside. Town is much more my sort of place.'

The Brigadier harrumphed. 'If you do not mind me saying, young Charlotte, you spent too much time careering around France in that ambulance of yours. Made you far too independent.'

'Well, I have to be, Uncle,' Lottie returned archly. 'With father dead and no brothers to inherit the title, I shall have to make my own way.'

'And very successful she is too.' Henry Blake touched her hand. 'Even if she too is an Honourable.' His eyes flashed with some emotion Melissa could not quite fathom as he glanced her way. Could he be, she wondered, a communist as well as a conscientious objector? Maybe just a socialist, like herself, she reasoned. No harm in that.

The conversation lapsed as the maid collected up the empty soup plates. Melissa glanced at her. She was unknown to her, perhaps drafted in from the village for the evening. She noticed that her uniform was rather too baggy and hoped fervently it was not a spare one of poor Meg's.

Smithers appeared with a huge salver, which he laid on the substantial oak sideboard.

'Excellent.' Brigadier Ferguson rubbed his hands. 'A real treat here for this course. Poole Harbour lobster.'

Oh Lord, thought Melissa. For Alasdair, this could turn out to be the meal from hell.

TWENTY-THREE

Smithers served Sir Reginald, then Melissa. He bent low close to Alasdair's ear and said, 'The cook has taken the liberty of loosening and preparing your lobster meat in the shell, sir.' He moved smoothly on.

Observing the exchange brought tears to Melissa's eyes. The staff really were so thoughtful; it was as though they were willing Alasdair to succeed. She moved to point out the long-handled lobster fork with its strange tines, but Alasdair had got there before her.

She looked across at the Countess, who was watching her with an inscrutable expression on her face. The Countess then made a point of turning to Sir Reginald, and she proceeded to work on charming him. Her voice was low and sultry and impossible for Melissa to overhear, much to her chagrin.

Determined not to fuss over Alasdair, her course finished – there really was not much in a lobster tail, after all – Melissa looked down the table. Arthur Baggeley seemed to be in a pole position. Rose was attempting to charm him; she had a low voice like the Countess, but she could not carry off the sultry manner that seemed to be the Countess's stock in trade. With Rose, it came over as though she was directing a hockey match. Too loud, too strident. Agnés, on his other side, seemed content to just listen, but every so often she dipped her head and looked up at Arthur through her admirable, long eyelashes with an effective winsome and enigmatic look. Melissa, watching Arthur's face, rather thought that it was Agnés who was catching his attention. She might have to revise her matchmaking plans. She was disturbed from her speculation when the dumb waiter came up with a clang.

The following course was Dorset lamb, tender and thinly sliced. Again, she noticed that slightly smaller pieces of meat had been positioned on Alasdair's plate. When the vegetables came round, both Smithers and the maid automatically served them onto Alasdair's plate as though it were silver service in a restaurant, rather than the usual help yourself for the rest of the guests as they came round.

However, she noticed, glancing at Alasdair, that she need not have worried about him this evening after all. He tucked into his food and appeared to be relaxed, happy to remain in his own thoughts, listening intently, a slight frown on his forehead, eating everything that had been given to him.

Melissa returned to her perusal of the Rose situation; she was still making the most of her seating and monopolising Arthur, giving that strange occasional bark of her laugh. This, of course, left Alasdair free from small talk from that side of the table. He remained there, brooding and silent, even between mouthfuls. She wondered if he was earwigging conversations around the table. She did hope so.

People often thought that blind people developed special senses and that their hearing developed somehow magically to compensate. It was not true, but without the stimulus of sight and the distractions that offered, a blind person had a tremendous capacity to focus the brain, and the so-called enhanced hearing was a reflection of that. Still, it was no bad thing, she reflected, if people at least respected Alasdair for his hearing.

Seeing that Bernard was sitting unoccupied, Melissa decided to try to engage him in conversation. She couldn't quite pinpoint why she was so wary of him. There was something repellent and reptilian about him. Even if he did remind her of a basking seal, oily and wet. It wasn't just the ingrained sense of entitlement that a wealthy and powerful man possessed. After all, Alasdair's father had it in spades, positioned as he was at the heart of the ruling class, but essentially he was a kind man. That was what was missing with Bernard Lyon. There was not an ounce of kindness in him. It was as if he were carved from rubber – slippery, cold, heartless – but she had to try, be brave. 'I believe that you are a banker? Is that correct?'

'Yes, investments are my line. Stocks and shares. Reginald can vouch for me.'

Melissa watched a flicker of annoyance pass across the Brigadier's face, but Bernard was either too pompous or thick-skinned to heed the warning. 'Who do you bank with?'

Melissa blinked. This was blunt, bordering on presumption. 'Coutts,' she stated coolly.

'Sound bank, aristocratic, of course, but safe, though you will not get big returns without a bit of a risk. Are you interested in investments?' Melissa looked at him wide-eyed and shook her head with a bit of a simper to try to deflect his lack of propriety.

'What about your father or your grandfather?' Bernard was relentless. Was he really going to discuss business over the dinner table?

'I believe they have their own people. It is not a subject we tend to converse on.'

'Quite right,' Brigadier Ferguson interjected. 'Business. Not a proper subject for the table, old boy, leave it out.'

'Indeed,' murmured the Countess, 'Dear Bernard, do not be so bourgeois.'

This clearly hit home, and he flushed. So there was some emotion in there, despite appearances. His large domed head was already glistening from the heat, and with his chubby face reddened, Melissa revised her opinion. Now he rather resembled a grilled tomato.

She smiled and tried another tack. 'Are you married, Bernard?' There was a spluttering sound from the Countess that turned into a cough.

'No, I have not had that pleasure.' He smiled but it appeared more of a grimace, belying his light response. 'Confirmed bachelor, I am afraid.'

'But she is right, you should marry, create a dynasty. For a man in your position, it is almost an imperative,' the Countess commented slyly.

'No, my dear, I am afraid I am quite determined. Matrimony is not for me.'

Melissa frowned. Was there some nuance here that she was missing? She looked across the table and saw Henry Blake was watching her. He smiled; he reminded her of a crocodile. Was it her he was contemplating snapping up or the banker?

'There seem to be an inordinate amount of confirmed bachelors at this table. What do you think, George?' Henry asked, raising his voice to carry across to the other side of the table. Melissa craned her neck around to look at Alasdair, as she just knew from the tone and expression on Henry's face that there was some devilment going on here.

George was sitting to the left of his Aunt Honor, who was seated at the far end of the long table. With the Georgian silver epergnes, candles and floral displays, Melissa thought idly that it was highly unlikely Honor could even see her husband at the far end of the table some twenty foot from her. What a lonely and exposed place it was as the hostess.

George coughed. 'Yes, but Henry, some of us are more confirmed than others, don't you know? Even those that do marry may only feel obliged.' A barb aimed at Rose? Was George jealous? Melissa cursed to herself; she just could not see around Alasdair without causing a fuss.

Lady Honor intervened. 'But surely, George, you will one day wish to be married?'

'Absolutely, Aunt, but rather like Bernard over there, I want to make my way first, although unlike Bernard, I positively yearn for the bliss of the matrimonial state.'

What on earth was he on about? Melissa was astonished. She felt a squeeze on her knee; she looked at Alasdair and he slightly shook his head. Taking the hint, she did not jump into the conversation as she might have wished. He might be her cousin, but, really, George could be a pompous ass.

The Dorset lamb was followed by New Forest raspberries, cream and meringue – a delightful concoction that melted in the mouth. The ladies then retired into the green drawing room for coffee. Melissa momentarily felt some sympathy with the pouting Countess. This really was a tedious convention and time it was dropped. Startled to find herself in such close accord with the Countess, Melissa was unable to settle. She glanced around, fidgeting; she was perching on the edge of a sofa. Lottie was at the far end, chatting to Rose. The Countess paced the room, smoking, as Agnés, her companion, hovered. Lady Honor was sitting magisterially on an upright chair. her thoughts her own.

Melissa tuned from the desultory conversation, just waiting for Alasdair to return. Would someone remember to help him? Should she go and check? In more light-hearted times, she would have indulged in a liqueur, or at least another cocktail, but she was cautious, feeling already slightly squiffy from the wine at dinner. It was, perhaps, the height of idiocy to dull the senses when there was a murderer on the loose. She noticed, however, that her other ladies were not quite so squeamish, and the maid assigned to the drawing room was doing a great run on the substantial number of liqueurs on offer this evening.

Coffee, cigars and port over, a time that seemed interminable to Alasdair, the conversation dominated by the Brigadier with a bee in his bonnet over local land rights and a surprisingly vocal Arthur, he was surprised when, as the men rose to leave, George appeared at his side and dug him in the ribs with his elbow. 'Take my arm. I want to have a chat with you. There is something you need to know. I need to get it off my chest.'

'Keep your voice down,' hissed Alasdair. 'Are you mad?'

'No, just determined. This bloody situation has to end.'

Alasdair caught hold of George's upper arm – too hard, in his agitation; under his fingers, he felt George wince. 'Where shall we go?' He was too wound up to apologise. What was George up to? Was he deliberately setting himself up as bait? Didn't he realise how dangerous this situation was?

'I suppose Maunedville has permanently sequestered the library. Let's go to Uncle Reggie's snug. He is bound to be too busy playing host to need it at the moment.'

Alasdair was furious. Never had he so much wished that he had his sight. It was unnerving to have a conversation that could be overheard and not to see who might be listening in. George was being reckless, a condition that never boded well, in his experience in the field. He remembered, suddenly, a situation in the war. He could almost smell the cordite, the memory was so strong. He had been following a group of Tommies; they were on their way to take possession of an abandoned section of German trench. Alasdair was there, intelligence gathering. Before he could stop them and advise caution, a group of the younger men, new recruits, fresh-faced and clean uniformed, broke off and ran forward in high spirits, jumped into the trench and began ransacking the area. The explosion that killed two of them and wounded six others, three eventually fatally, was a carefully hidden booby trap left behind by the Germans to inflict maximum damage and destroy any evidence useful to the enemy. A waste of life that weighed heavily on Alasdair's conscience. In future, although only attached to squads as an 'advisor', he always made sure he led from the front. A habit that was popular with the troops but that would have appalled the higher ups, the loss of an intelligence officer being considered the loss of a far more valuable asset.

Meanwhile, he was aware that they had walked down a few corridors before George dipped to open a door. He led Alasdair into the room and to a wing-backed chair next to another fireplace. Once sitting down, Alasdair became aware of the heat and crackle of the fire; he moved his head and he caught it on a wing. A smaller chair than in the library, then. A similar set-up, Alasdair surmised, to the library but probably on a smaller scale. He wished he had paid more attention earlier in the day. He was going to have to spend some time getting his bearings or he would never cope in this house. In the flat in town, he could rest his hand on any surface. Navigate a room without trouble. Open a cupboard and find what he wanted. Here, he was lost, and it disturbed him.

'Ho, ho, here is where he keeps his good spirits. Fancy a brandy or a whisky? My God, he has a Glenmorangie here.'

Alasdair nodded vigorously in assent. He could hear the clink of glass and the gurgle of poured liquid, and he thought he almost detected the distinctive smell of the malt as George's footsteps approached. 'Look the thing is—' George began.

There was a draft as though a window or door had been opened quietly. 'What the …' George exclaimed, then there was a crack, a heavy thud, and silence.

TWENTY-FOUR

Alasdair sat very still, all senses on alert. Time seemed to expand as he listened. Silence. No movement. A rustle of clothing? He attempted to still his breathing, which appeared so loud that it threatened to mask all other sounds. Someone was coming towards him. This was it. He waited to die. There was a flutter of light movement close to his face. A hint of a body smell. A wisp of fabric brushed his face. He started back. A low, deep, almost indiscernible chuckle, and then silence, another waft of air, and the click of a door.

Alasdair rose cautiously to his feet. Where was George? What had happened? He had a very bad feeling. It reminded him of something else. He dismissed the thought. No time for that. Slowly, he edged forward, small step by small step. His foot made contact with something soft on the floor. He knelt down; it was a body. Afraid to move it in case he did any further damage, he felt around, found an arm, felt for the wrist. There was a pulse. Faint, but there. Abandoning all caution, he yelled for help and kept yelling, his brush with death pumping the adrenaline to feed his voice.

There was a cacophony of heavy footsteps in the hall

and the door burst open and crashed against a piece of furniture, startling Alasdair into a standing position.

It was Maundeville who took charge; he led Alasdair back to a chair and fetched him a brandy this time. He sent Smithers to arrange for the doctor to be called.

Alasdair described what had happened. Maundeville confirmed that it was George who had been attacked. He was alive but had been hit on the back of the head and could not be roused.

'Different MO then?' Alasdair commented.

'Yes, but he or she may have had no time to equip themselves with the knife. Did he manage to tell you anything?'

'You heard that he was going to then?'

'Hard to miss it. Damn fool. Would be hard to place who didn't. Even some of the women were milling around.'

'I got nothing.' Fear had turned to anger. George had been such an idiot, and Alasdair was damned if another of Mellie's cousins was going to die.

'Well, keep that under your hat for the moment. We may be able to use it.'

'What, use me as bait?' Alasdair grumbled but not too seriously; he was flattered at the obvious confidence being shown in him. Perhaps, just perhaps, there could be a life for him. Could it be that he was not quite as useless as he thought? From the sound of Maundeville's voice, he could tell that he was serious and not just humouring him. But what could his future be? This incident showed that whatever happened, his would be a life of danger. Even walking in the park was fraught with obstacles. He did have skills, though, and he needed to use them and let go of what might have been.

George was in luck. The doctor, a sensible-looking, bluff and hale hearty type in tweeds and brogues, arrived within twenty minutes. He ushered everyone from the room, with the exception of Maundeville, Alasdair, who was still cradling his brandy, and Melissa, sitting at his feet, clutching his knee.

The doctor thoroughly examined his patient, opened his medical bag and began swathing George's head in bandages.

'All I can do pro tem,' he stated. He had a steady, calm voice with a hint of the Hampshire accent. 'He has not come round, and that is worrying. I suspect a fractured skull. He needs transferring to the cottage hospital as soon as possible. Do you have a motor here?'

Maundeville looked nonplussed. 'What? Don't you have one?'

'Dear me no. On my income? I came in the pony and trap, but it is ten miles to the hospital and would be a rough journey in my trap. I could not guarantee he'd survive.'

'George has a large motor. We could use that,' Melissa said. 'I think mine might be too small.'

'Yes, but who the hell will drive it?' Alasdair put a restraining hand on Melissa's shoulder. In a moment of clarity and revelation, he realised that even with all his confidence and optimism, he would still need her as his guide, partner and love. To lose her would be far worse, even, than losing his sight. It gave him, all in that moment, a sense of purpose, of duty, of interdependency. They were a unit, just like in the war, and he needed to forget about himself now and pour all his abilities, honour and, yes, love into this unit, and this unit alone.

'I need you here with me.' His voice was firm. It brooked no contradiction. The last thing they needed now was for her to leap off and leave him. But she clearly had no such idea; the pressure on his knee tightened.

'What about Henry and Lottie? They both drove ambulances in the war – a motor should be no problem and they must be expert in handling the wounded.'

'That could work,' the doctor conceded. 'They can follow me in the trap. As I said, I could take him in the back. I have had to with emergencies in the past, but with a head injury, we are in dangerous territory.'

Maundeville prevaricated. 'But they might be suspects. There is no way George can be involved in my show.'

The doctor frowned, perplexed at the other man's attitude. 'Time is of the essence, man.'

'Oh, very well. Melissa, you go summon them, and the Brigadier as well.'

She pulled Alasdair to his feet. 'Not without you,' she whispered, her lips brushing his ear. 'I am not letting you out of my sight from now on. We are in this together or not at all.'

Melissa was proud of her family when she recalled events later. Henry and Lottie showed their true colours, helping fashion a stretcher and staying calm, with Lottie assuming nursing duties.

Henry went out and collected George's car and brought it to the front of the house. Henry, Maundeville, the doctor and Reginald brought George out on the stretcher. 'Lottie, sit in the back. We can rest his head on your lap. What we need is a pillow.'

Lottie produced one from behind her back and a blanket.

'Good girl,' the doctor said approvingly.

'Look, Edward,' Brigadier Ferguson addressed the doctor. 'You go in the front with Henry, quicker that way, it would be damned slow following you in the trap. Poor boy. I cannot lose another.' He grimaced, and his eyes watered. 'I'll stir Davies and get him to follow you in the trap to the hospital. Then you, Henry and Lottie can bring Davies back with you later.'

'Sounds an excellent plan.' The doctor clapped his arm on Brigadier Ferguson's shoulder. They were clearly old friends. 'I'll do my best and stay with him. This way we can go by the water splash. It will be quicker.'

Then they were off, Henry driving, the doctor beside him in the front and Lottie with a still unconscious George in the back, his head resting on the pillow in her lap.

'Telephone, won't you?' Brigadier Ferguson's voice trembled and then he coughed and recovered. Melissa took Alasdair's hand, rested it on her arm and threaded her other arm through her uncle's. Giving it a squeeze, she reached up and kissed his cheek.

'He'll be fine,' she said with more firmness than she felt. 'We always said George was thick-skinned and bear-headed.' Her attempt at a joke paid off as Brigadier Ferguson gave a quick laugh and then dropped her arm as they made their way into the house through the scullery door, it being too narrow for three. Melissa squeezed Alasdair's arm to indicate the small opening and muttered, 'Crocodile.' He fell in behind her, still clutching her free arm for guidance.

When they were back in the drawing room, he turned

to Melissa and said in a low voice, 'What entrance to the house was that we came through?'

'The scullery,' she whispered back.

'Tomorrow morning you are taking me for a full recce of the whole house. I want to know every entrance and possible exit. I need to get a plan of the house into my head. I cannot hope to solve what is happening without it.'

They had no further time for consultation, as Maundeville had gathered everyone back into the drawing room, servants as well. It was crowded, and Alasdair could almost smell the undercurrent of fear. He sighed. It was the trenches all over again. Would he never be rid of it? He clenched his fist as he realised his right hand was trembling. He knew that he had come very close to death tonight, as close a shave as when he had been injured and lost his sight. Why had he been spared? It was an uncomfortable feeling to consider that the killer may have thought he was too pathetic to kill. All his former confidence left him with a whoosh as the adrenaline he had been cruising on spluttered away, leaving only darkness. He straightened his fingers; well, he was not going to let himself be a washout. Innocuous they may think him, but he was bloody well going to show them otherwise.

TWENTY-FIVE

Maundeville and Brigadier Ferguson were again left to try to instil order into the house party. Watching the scene, Melissa saw that, to be fair, the servants were silent. They looked frightened, but with their servants' training were determined not to show it. Melissa was struck at just how few there were. She worked on identifying them. With her red hands and damp apron, the small mousey woman, almost as wide as she was tall, with a ruddy face, could only be the scullery woman fresh from her task of washing the dishes. Melissa had not met her, and to her shame could not recall her name or whether she lived in or came up from the village. She suspected the latter. Next to her was Mrs Davenport, the housekeeper, who did live in; she had been remarkably in the background over the weekend. Perhaps she was doubling up with some of the staff. The mechanics of the weekend had certainly gone smoothly. It could not be easy catering for such a large number.

The cook, Mrs Smithers, the butler's wife, certainly lived in. Beside her was the parlour maid, who had doubled up serving at dinner and then afterwards the coffee and liqueurs.

The idle thought crept in that she must be very overworked at the moment with Meg gone. Not only would she have to see to the female guests but also all the extra duties. Perhaps they got in extra help from the village when necessary, as next to her was a very nervous young woman in an ill-fitting maid's uniform, her hair not quite right and her hands revealing the hard work she was generally used to. Melissa recognised her from dinner. Drafted in at short notice, Melissa suspected. All this she would have to investigate and take control of, if they were to settle living here. It was clear that something was badly needed. If her uncle did have money, why on earth was he not spending it on the staff? There must be many women in the surrounding villages that could do with the work – so few men had come home from the war, leaving great holes in family incomes.

In sharp contrast to the servants lined up like mute swans, the guests were running amok. Melissa would have been amused in other circumstances. Henry Blake was insisting that Scotland Yard be called in immediately rather than waiting for Monday. Maundeville was prevaricating. Melissa noted with surprise that Bernard Lyon was protesting this idea, in sharp contrast to his earlier fears for his safety; surely the police were a safe option? He was being backed up shrilly by the Countess, two high spots of colour on her cheekbones. 'The police? Sacré bleu! Never, never have I been mixed up with such as them. Maundeville, it is you must deal with this.'

Melissa wondered cynically if the Countess thought Maundeville was an easier foil, but contrary to that, if she was a spy, would she not want the police called to take the heat off her?

Maundeville looked to Brigadier Ferguson, who shrugged. Melissa thought her uncle looked unwell; his skin was pale and he had that green-about-the-gills look that tended to foretell medical problems. She had seen enough of it during her medical visiting – all the family had allowed her to do during the war. No rushing off to drive ambulances for her. No, she visited the young wounded officers in the hospital, wrote letters and read to them. The fact that many of them were swathed in head bandages, effectively blind if not actually medically so, was an irony that was not lost on her later when Alasdair returned so late in the war, himself blinded permanently.

Lady Honor, standing beside her husband, must have felt the same way, as in an unprecedented show of intimacy in public, she put her arm through his and squeezed his upper arm with the other, offering support at a time of trial. 'We are all tired,' she stated. 'I suggest that we retire for bed. We can discuss things better tomorrow morning, in a calmer and more lucid way after a good night's rest.'

There were a few half-hearted objections from the group, but on the whole, a tacit consent. The more so when she added, 'Besides, there are no trains to or from London until the morning anyway. And then it is only a Sunday service.'

'A good plan, Lady Honor.' Maundeville seemed to have pulled himself together; for a moment there, Melissa thought he had looked rattled. There was certainly no support to be had from Brigadier Ferguson at this time. No, Maundeville was back to being forceful – he assumed command. 'Everyone go to bed, lock your doors, and if any of you are thinking of leaving, think again. Anyone leaving will be seen as suspect number one.' The room emptied with an unnatural haste, the guests now unusually quiet and sombre.

At last there was just Maundeville, Alasdair and Melissa. Even Godfrey Greenwood had scuttled off. Melissa had made quite a show of getting Alasdair out of the chair as a delaying tactic, applying pressure on his arm as a warning that she hoped he picked up. She turned and looked at Maundeville expectantly, noticing for the first time that now the room had emptied and his face rested into its more natural lines rather than his role, he too was looking his age this late in the evening. How old was he? He must be sixty if he was a day. 'Not now,' he muttered with a dismissive flick of his wrist. 'We will reconvene in the library at ten tomorrow morning.' So, rather disconsolately, Melissa led Alasdair out of the room and up the stairs to their bedroom.

As soon as she had opened the door, Alasdair was past her. He made unerringly for the bed, sat on the end and leant forward, his head in his hands. He rested there for a moment; he appeared to be stilling his breathing. Melissa, realising he needed time, tiptoed over to one of the dainty chintz chairs in the window recess and sat quietly, resisting all the questions that tumbled into her mind. This was a stance she recognised. One she knew from the early dark days after he returned from St Dunstan's Rehabilitation Unit. If this weekend set him back to his former torment, she would not be able to forgive herself. She had hoped he was through this. She stopped and considered what might have happened in that room with George. She shuddered, suddenly cold, stood up and took her red wool shawl off the back of the dressing table chair and wrapped it around her tightly as if trying to take comfort as well as warmth.

Alasdair continued to remain as he was, the time stretching like a taut wire, fighting clearly for his composure, and then he stretched up and flopped backwards onto the bed with a sigh. His eyes opened. 'Well, that was fun.'

Melissa sucked her breath in, unsure how to respond. It was like walking on thin ice when he was like this – a false step and she would be frozen out. 'Fun?' she ventured.

'Yes, about as much fun as going over the top.'

Melissa hated it when he was in this mood: this throwaway flippancy with the edge of desperation, even despair. She so wanted to make it better but seemed to lack the skills. When she encouraged him to talk about the war, he clammed up, and as for feelings, well, that was clearly a bridge too far. It was stiff upper lip all the way. But he did tell her he loved her. That was a start. She had more than many of her friends had. She had a husband who loved her. Many of them were widowed or had lost loved ones in the war; others were unable to find a partner in peace time, so rare were eligible men. Her cousin Charlotte was right about that, and look at Rose – desperation leaked from every pore. She was lucky. She had to keep reminding herself that. And she did love him so much. There had been talk among her friends in London, the fast, brittle type who mentioned the cripples, the fiancés who had returned too damaged to take back. The whispered talk of private nursing homes, of sanatoriums. Sons hidden away from prying eyes. The limbless, mutilated beggars on street corners, glanced at, a quick shudder and then forgotten. Yes, she had been lucky, and now she had nearly lost him again.

'What happened in that room?' She tried again.

Alasdair hauled himself up the bed and propped himself against the headboard using the pillows. 'George was about to tell me something, something he thought important. The bloody fool told me in front of a roomful of people that he wanted to tell me something.'

'When? Which people?' If only she had been there, would she have been able to prevent this?

'I don't bloody know, how can I?' Alasdair began, his voice rising. 'No, sorry, darling, you are right, thank you. I must stay calm, think.' There was a pause. He breathed in deeply and let it out loudly. 'It was after port and cigars.'

'So only the men could be in the room?'

'Yes, of course, you are right. But I could not tell you who may have left before George spoke to me. He was mad, mad. It was as if he wanted to provoke just such an outcome.'

Melissa winced at the pain in his voice. 'And then what happened?'

'We went to the Brigadier's study. George found the Glenmorangie, then someone must have come into the room there was a thud and then ... nothing.'

Melissa knew him too well; she recognised the prevarication. 'Then nothing what?'

'All right. He then came up to me. I was sitting in one of the chairs, George was bringing over my drink, there was a heavy thud, presumably George hitting the rug. Thank God for that. At least his landing was soft.'

'Yes, but what did he do when he came up to you?'

'There was a pause. I was sure I was a goner, then a waft

of air, and then a low chuckle. I think he was playing with me, enjoying himself.'

'Or just checking you really could not see him.'

'What do you mean?'

Melissa stood up, went over to Alasdair and waved her hand, palm away from her, across his face as though she too were testing his eyes for sight.

'What? What did you do? That was it exactly. A waft of air.'

'I was waving my hand across your face to see if you could see it. That is what he must have done – not close enough to touch you but close enough to be sure that you could not see anything. You realise that being blind saved your life?' She shivered, colder air like icy fingers probing deep into her bones. She stood up and went over to the fire, raking the ashes until she had a glow and throwing on a few small logs. Anything to stave off the icy fear that clutched at her.

'I'm not sure that counts as a plus. Too useless to be a threat and not worth killing.' Perversely, he sounded morose.

'But don't you see? You are not useless. You keep saying he. How do you know?' The ice receded as the flames of inspiration caught her.

'Well, I just assumed.'

'Or do you know? What is it you sensed?' She persisted, brushing off her shawl in excitement. It lay pooled on the floor like blood.

Alasdair paused and thought for a moment. 'Well, it must have been only men who overheard what George said to me.'

'Yes, but that is a deduction. In that moment, the moment the murderer stood in front of you, what did you sense? Hear, feel, smell?' There was a pause.

'No perfume.' Alasdair smiled, his voice triumphant.

TWENTY-SIX

Alasdair's mind began to race. He massaged his temples with his fingers. He needed to be calm. These damn useless eyes – what help could he really be to the service? What had he been thinking? He was just a burden, a sea anchor, pulling them all down. If he could have found who it was who had whacked him and blinded him back then, then he could understand the motive for murder all right. The savage thought pulled him out of the doldrums. 'Melissa, quick, your notebook. List the men.' He began to tick them off on his fingers. 'We have Maundeville, Godfrey Greenwood, Henry Blake, Brigadier Ferguson, Arthur Baggeley, Bernard Lyon and the vicar, Harold James.'

'We can cross off quite a few of those, surely?'

'I do not think so. Think. This is another member of the family, brother to the first victim. George and Emma must have definitely been up to something.' He frowned; he was convinced this was the essence of the case.

'What on earth could it be? I cannot believe they could have been up to anything that warranted murder? Could they have got into something deeper than they understood?

There is that link to Bernard Lyon. Is he under suspicion of spying as well as the Countess? They appear rather thick. They clearly know each other. You said that he also telephoned Brigadier Ferguson and cadged an invite this weekend.'

'Hmm, but just because he is a profiteering banker does not mean we should be influenced to fit him to the crime. Disliking someone who you find morally repugnant does not make them a murderer.' Alasdair found it very hard to believe that such a prominent man would risk all he had by committing the desperate act of murder. He also could not believe that the great sweating lump that Melissa had described him as would have the energy or the strength to carry it out. On the other hand, he had that cold, calculating brain. A mind that had no conscience, happy to profit off the back of thousands of dead men lost in the fields of Flanders.

'Oh, very well, another angle then. Do any of the men use cologne, pomade?'

'Good God. I hope not.' He sounded genuinely horrified.

Melissa's lips twitched, 'You can be so old-fashioned sometimes, darling.' She paused. 'Bernard Lyon might.'

'Mellie, stop it. It doesn't do to focus on one person. It skews the investigation. That is where Maundeville has been going wrong – he has spent too much time on the Countess.' The last thing he wanted was Melissa anywhere near that man. Her perception was right: lard he might be, but dangerous. There was a nasty spike buried there waiting to catch the unwary.

'All right, but do you recognise the smell of any of the

men? Could you identify them from that moment in the study?'

'No, I have been too busy this weekend with not slipping up and making a fool of myself.' Would he ever be able to let that pride go? It was utterly exhausting attempting to keep up appearances. The amount of energy it took to bend his will to increase his concentration, his senses, training them to work overtime, and what for? To pass muster at a country house weekend with family? But then it wasn't just family, was it? This was it – the Brigadier was offering him a lifeline. Melissa was right. He had exhausted his bounds at the flat in London. He couldn't tell her, but he now felt penned in, a delightful prison but a prison none the less. He had to do something. He thought back to the classes at St Dunstan's. The classes he had rejected – and, as an officer, they had let him. Woodworking, furniture-caning, basket-weaving. Yes, he could rustle up a set of cane-seated bistro chairs, but what use was that in this life? However, they had created maps. Maps using glue and string to raise the features and let his fingers find the contours. That is what he needed. A floor plan of every wing of the house. Every room if necessary.

'Yes, but we ought to try now,' Melissa said. 'Sniff the person out.'

He heard the attempt at humour and admired her the more for it. She was good for him, but she needed caution.

'Yes, but with subtlety. If the murderer thinks we are searching for him, we will be in serious danger. Fluffy aristo and blind idiot, remember? You cannot have it both ways, and I suspect he will be watching me.'

'I just had a thought. What if a woman did not use perfume? It could have been one of the ladies.'

'But that would mean she would have to be tipped off by one of the men. I am not sure there was time, Mellie.'

She sighed. 'Unless she was listening at the door. I will have to think who was with the ladies in the drawing room.'

Alasdair heard the frustration and tiredness in that sigh. He felt the guilt creep in again; it was his fault she was so tired – that damn sea anchor dragging them back. 'Enough now, let us try and get some sleep and be fresh for the morning. I assume Thomas has left everything ready.

'Yes, all done.'

'Wait, before you get into bed, take the dressing table chair and jam the handle under the door knob. I assume you have locked the door?'

'Yes, but do you think this is really necessary?'

'Oh yes. These old houses, you know. I would not be surprised if the keys fit many of the locks, especially on this floor. Make no mistake – there is someone very dangerous on the prowl and they will apparently stop at nothing to protect themselves. Assuming we have just one murderer, he has two, possibly three, deaths under his belt now.' They say it gets easier after the first kill. Had he found it so? Yes, you could only kill by distancing yourself, terming the target as just that – a target, not a human, not a living and breathing man or woman. He had seen some men, though, during the war that loved to kill; they seemed to thrill at the work. Kept a score card. He resisted a shudder. Heaven help them if they had one of them here.

'Don't say that. Poor George. No matter what we think of him, I still love him. He is my cousin. He must survive, he must.' She sounded wounded.

'You are extraordinary, you know? Such a huge capacity

for compassion and love.' He kissed her. He felt Melissa smile and then she yawned.

'All this sleuthing is exhausting.' She rolled over and was soon deeply asleep.

Alasdair caught some sleep early on in the night and then awoke in the early hours. He lay there pondering the new suspects.

Were all three murders connected? He corrected himself – two murders and an attempted murder. What was it that Emma knew that had got her killed? What could she possibly know that was so dangerous? He thought back to his encounters with Emma in the past. To be fair, he had not met her much, because the war had got in the way. She had always seemed a quiet thing, quite in the shadow of her brother, George, and her confident, ebullient cousins on Mellie's side. Being the grandchildren of an earl had that effect. Alasdair's father had always bemoaned the overconfidence of the aristocracy, the unalienable belief that they were right and could do what they wanted with impunity. Sadly, he reflected, the success of his father proved this was all too often correct.

But back to Emma. Was she the type that sat around quietly and picked things up? Had she and George been involved in a spot of blackmail and bitten off more than they could chew? That trail led to Bernard Lyon – George had admitted as much to them – so what was it George had wanted to say last night? Another plot?

Emma had also worked at the charity Bernard Lyon was involved with. Another link to the banker, but when Alasdair thought of Lyon, he gained the impression of a tall, overweight, blustering coward. That lump of lard. Not a likely suspect as a murderer. However, he thought back to his conversation with Brigadier Ferguson. Why had Bernard Lyon wanted to be here this weekend? Who had driven him off the road? What was his link to the Countess? And what had he said to the Brigadier about her? Alasdair needed to find out.

He thought again of that scene in the study with George. Whoever it was had to be light of foot. He was sure of that. They had taken George by surprise. Thinking back, he also remembered one other thing. He was almost certain that now Mellie had mentioned it, Bernard Lyon wore some sort of cologne. Big men often did, to mask other odours. Yes, a cologne, something expensive, something French? Almost feminine. His mind played over that for a moment of two. An idea formed.

Then there was the other thing he could not remember detecting. The smell of cigarettes. Henry Blake positively reeked, and most of the men had been smoking cigars after dinner. Should he not have been able to smell cigar smoke? He had never thought about it before. Confusion and then self-doubt crept into his mind. He ought to know – two years spent in rehabilitation at St Dunstan's and then wasted as he spent the intervening years feeling sorry for himself in the flat. Three wasted years, deluding himself that he could cope. The early hours were not usually kind to the tormented soul, but as if something somewhere recognised his need, sleep came, and he dozed again for a few hours.

It was with some surprise, therefore, that he was awoken by Mellie. 'Come on, Alasdair, wake up. It's Sunday. We have breakfast and church to go to and we need to progress the notebook. Oh, and the timeline you mentioned on the blackboard.'

'Oh blast, do we have to go to church? We need the time to sort out the suspects.'

'Of course we must go. If you are even contemplating settling here we will have to be part of the parish.'

'You like the idea, don't you?'

'To be blunt, yes. There is so much space here. The staff seem accommodating and symp— helpful to you. I suppose it rather hinges on whether you feel you can work with Davies and Brigadier Ferguson. Oh gosh, even I am calling him that now.'

'It does still suit him. I wouldn't be surprised if Honor doesn't call him that as well.'

Melissa laughed. 'And?' she prompted. 'What do you think?'

He was aware that she was holding her breath. 'Assuming this is solved before Special Branch arrive, we could stay on for a bit and work things out. We can hardly make a decision at the moment with the house in uproar. Who knows, all the servants or Davies might not want to stay on in a house where murders have taken place.'

'Oh, we must find out about George, how could I forget?' Her voice wobbled. 'What if he is dead? Oh dear, I think I am going to cry.'

TWENTY-SEVEN

SUNDAY BREAKFAST

Alasdair realised with a pang that he had not really considered her feelings, so caught up was he in his own. Where had he been these last years? Why on earth had she stayed with him? Why had she not rebelled? They did not even have children to occupy her. Perhaps looking after him was a full-time job? She had never mentioned children. He did not deserve her. He must make it up to her and make this move work – if it was offered. Well, he would make sure it was. It was the least he could do for her.

It also occurred to him that it was unusual for her to awake this bright and so early. Had she not slept? Normally in the evening she loved her cocktails and wine with dinner. This meant that usually she slept deeply but did wake up more than a little hazy on occasion. It was galling to consider that, once again, he had no idea what his wife had drunk last night. Most husbands, of course, would just have observed, made a comment, but he could not. Was it something you could ask a wife? Did he need to pay more attention?

It was not until this moment that he considered what a

change there had been in their marriage since he had come home from the war. Not only for him, but also her. He pondered the need for a conversation at some point. His mind shied away from it. No. Let us get the murderer out of the way first.

When they entered the dining room for breakfast, Melissa exclaimed that there was no one there. Alasdair flipped open his watch and felt for the hands. 'Mellie, it is seven o'clock, you chump. Any sensible person is still wrapped up in bed.'

'Oh, let us do the opposite. Go for a walk. The sun is coming up. I cannot just sit around. I need some exercise.'

A short time later, bundled in their heavy outdoor coats taken from a hall closet, they set forth. They collected Sheba from her stable home and set off in the direction of the New Forest surrounding the estate.

The sun rose slowly. The forest was crisp with white frost. Fingers of sunlight crept between the trees, creating light but as yet no heat. The grass crunched under foot, releasing a mild boggy smell.

Alerted by an almost imperceptible impulse, Alasdair turned his face to the sun, closed his eyes and allowed the fingers to caress his face. The glare disorientated him when he opened his eyes. He stumbled. How was it, he thought, that he could not see, but at the same time was affected by glare? He could feel Melissa watching him. It was uncanny, now he was blind – that almost sixth sense one had that someone was staring at you. It made you turn your head to look, and often you'd catch a stranger looking away just as you turned; this sense was very strong in him now. Was it paranoia? Or was it genuine? As if in answer, Mellie squeezed his arm.

He really should ask her to dig out his dark glasses, then he paused. That almost ubiquitous sign, coupled with the white stick of the many blind ex-servicemen. At St Dunstan's it was encouraged, but Alasdair always felt it was more to save the embarrassment of the sighted than to protect the blind. It was a badge, a symbol to the world of his disability, but he had not wanted it to define him. Should he cave in or would he resist as he had so much over recent years, refusing to give an inch and bow to the inevitable? What had he achieved? He sighed. No, not the inevitable, but the conventional? The insidious perception of the nation of what a blind man should conform to. Well, he would damn well resist. He was not going to be a norm, never would be.

'You know,' he commented. 'I think we should dig out my desert sunglasses. Much as I appreciate the odd glimpses of light, the glare is quite impossible sometimes.'

'What an awfully good idea, darling.' Alasdair heard the surprise and caution in her voice. 'I must remember to carry them in future. Do you have an inside pocket in that coat? I am sure we have them with us packed away somewhere in the luggage. You know Thomas – he is frightfully efficient.'

'Yes, but perhaps not for church, hmm?' He was not quite ready for that. 'Come on, lead on, let us work off some of the breakfast we are about to indulge in.'

The woods smelt peaty, and the falling leaves rustled under foot. Melissa had set quite a pace and he realised how unfit he was. He persevered for a short while longer but became so hot, bundled up in his coat, and so out of breath that he called a halt. Melissa led him over to a fallen tree and they sat on the horizontal trunk. Melissa seemed happy to let the silence of the forest surround them. But then it was not silent; Alasdair could hear the rustle as the light breeze lifted the leaves in the treetops and stirred the loose leaves at their feet. He reached out, took off his glove and rested his hand on the trunk. It was dry from age but damp from the cool autumn air. He picked at the bark; it released a smell that all at once threw him back into the war – pine needles. He and two others had been on the trail of a deserter. A deserter or a spy? Either way, he was headed towards the German lines and their job was to apprehend the chap before he got there. Alive, if possible, only for the information. Regardless, it would be a firing squad later. This was a part of his job he hated. The generals saw spies everywhere, probably to explain away their own incompetence; it couldn't possibly be their fault, could it? So far, Alasdair had found no spies, only frightened, exhausted and witless men, driven mad by the guns, death and squalor. He suddenly hoped they did not find the deserter. Then a shot rang out. Alasdair had been kneeling behind a fallen tree, looking for boot prints. He turned. One of his team was down. Craig, a canny Scot who had enlisted early and had, until now, led a charmed life scratch-free. A clear shot through the head. This was a marksman. A German sniper, or had their man a rifle and wits after all?

Crouching, Alasdair searched the woods for the man with the gun. He was cautious about using his field glasses as there was still enough light that the glass might pick up and reflect, making him an easy target. He glanced over at his other team member, Adrian Masters, a young officer, a new recruit, raw and unpractised. He had been desperate to be included in this sortie. He wanted to be tested; well, now he was. He crouched behind a tree and was pulling out his field glasses. Alasdair called a warning and a bullet pinged into the fallen tree he was sheltering behind, releasing the smell of the sap. Strong, tart, head-clearing. With clarity, Alasdair realised that their assailant was up a tree. He waved at Adrian to keep down, but the young fool ignored him and decided to make a run for it over to where Alasdair was sheltering. Too late; the sniper was skilled well enough. He had the reach with the bullet finding the tree trunk. Another head shot and the poor young chump was dead.

Alasdair was furious. He wanted to leap up and charge down this killer of innocent young boys, but he didn't. He lowered himself to the ground and lay there. The sniper might have him in his sights but he, in turn, now knew which tree he was hiding in. The guns had stopped and there was silence throughout the forest, just the rustling and scratchings. All Alasdair had to do was wait. At some point, the sniper would have to descend the tree, and he would be waiting. This was now a duel to the death.

'Alasdair, Alasdair.' He was being shaken awake. Good God, had he missed him? He blinked and then was back, unaware of the shock in Melissa's eyes.

'Sorry, what?'

'You suddenly shot off the trunk and crouched down, covering your head with your hands, and then lay there. Are you all right, darling? Speak to me.'

He cleared his throat, embarrassed at being caught out. These episodes happened sporadically; they had been well-hidden from Melissa but Thomas knew of them. The doctors said they would fade, flashback episodes common among soldiers, a mere coping mechanism, nothing to worry about, go away, get on with life, forget them. But how could he forget them? When a blind man had flashbacks in colour, his vision was momentarily restored.

'I get flashbacks. They appear very real. It was the smell of the pine that set it off.'

'A flashback? To the war? What happened?'

'I killed a man.' He stood up, brushed himself down and reached for her arm. 'Come on, I am starving. Time for breakfast.'

This time when they approached the dining room, their faces flushed from the outdoors, it was after nine, and it seemed that every guest and member of the household had decided to grace the room with their presence that morning. Indeed, the hubbub of animated conversation could be heard in the hallway.

Melissa pushed the door open and was relieved to see two chairs vacant at the near end of the table. Either by luck or by design, they found themselves seated between Brigadier Ferguson and Maundeville. She guided Alasdair to a seat and sat down beside him. She felt that someone had punched her in the chest. To see Alasdair like that was so traumatic. He had never mentioned it. He had hidden it. What else had he hidden? She couldn't look at him; she was afraid she would cry. She turned instead to Brigadier Ferguson and looked expectantly at him, raising her eyebrows.

'Ah yes, my dear, George has passed a fair night at the cottage hospital, but he has not regained consciousness.'

'Oh dear. That is worrying, isn't it?' How many men had Alasdair killed? Could you ask your husband something like that? By the way, darling, how many men is it you have killed? She shivered.

'Actually, not so much,' interrupted Lottie, her eyes kind. 'Often, a coma is a blessing as it keeps the head still and helps the healing.' She stopped abruptly. 'But that doesn't mean that he is out of the woods yet,' she finished rather lamely.

'Will he be safe at the hospital?' Alasdair asked Maundeville quietly.

'Yes, the constable is on guard there for the moment and the staff have been alerted to watch out for visitors.'

'Good. We do not want someone attempting to finish the job, do we?'

'Just so.' Maundeville raised his voice somewhat. 'Although, as George was hit on the back of the head from behind, I imagine he has absolutely no idea who attacked him.' His voice was firm. 'Now, Alasdair, I wonder if I could persuade you and your wife to forego church. I want some more family information which I think you may be able to help me with, and you look like you are going to be late anyway.'

'Well, of course, sir,' Alasdair replied in mock deprecation. Melissa had to firmly resist a smile. He really was a devil. She hoped he had not laid it on too thickly, but Alasdair had achieved exactly what he wanted. However, she acknowledged that they really did need to talk to Maundeville. It was all getting overwhelming. Not least that she was concerned at what both of them had been keeping from her. Was it really all covered by state secrets? She sincerely hoped that he at least would be able to fill in some of the gaps. Maundeville was making a big show about the family, but she really couldn't think it was one of them. She looked at Maundeville with new eyes.

Had he killed men? Was that their job? The killing of men?

She looked further down the table and saw that even the Countess had deigned to get up for breakfast. Had she foregone her sleeping pills last night? Henry Blake, sitting next to Lottie, looked sombre, but he winked at Melissa and slightly shook his head. Bernard Lyon was at the far end of the table, talking animatedly to Lady Honor; he clearly was being charming as Honor laughed at some remark he had made. He had Godfrey Greenwood next to him. He, in turn, seemed to be in a dark mood, picking at his meal, his eyes on the plate, isolating himself. Next to him, Rose was also looking glum. Was she missing George? Arthur Baggeley? It was impossible to tell. Perhaps, at last, she had realised she should at least attempt to project some sort of mourning for the dead. After all, Emma was supposedly about to be her sister-in-law.

Further up the table was the Countess's companion, Agnés, who Melissa thought had suspiciously red eyes. Perhaps the result from another haranguing from the Countess? How ghastly to be reduced to such a level and have to work for so beastly a woman. However, to what lengths might she go to escape that life? It was a thought.

TWENTY-EIGHT

After an excellent full English breakfast, most of which Melissa assumed came from the farm or local provisioners, they made their way to the library to meet with Maundeville.

Godfrey Greenwood was there as well, shuffling through papers and buff folders. Melissa saw with amusement that many of them had 'Top Secret' emblazoned on them in red ink. It was almost an invitation to snoop. Maundeville seemed irritable. He asked Greenwood to leave with a lack of courtesy that startled her, expelling a plume of smoke, then stubbing out his cigarette and instantly lighting another from a silver cigarette box on his desk with a matching lighter that looked like it was heavy enough to be a weapon. Melissa coughed.

Maundeville's grumpiness may have startled Godfrey as well as he said rather testily, 'Yes, sir, I am just about to leave. One moment.' He reshuffled some papers and, with a curious glance at Melissa and Alasdair, left the room, closing the door with a snap.

Maundeville let silence surround them for a few minutes and then sighed. 'So, where are we?'

'First, while I remember it, what is the background to Greenwood?' Alasdair's voice had an eagerness in it that Melissa had not heard for a long while.

'Your reason for asking?' Maundeville was terse.

'I have just realised what has been troubling me. It has been buzzing around in the back of my mind. There is an occasional Teutonic cadence to his speech.'

'I believe his background is Belgian.'

'What? Like Agnés Baume?' Melissa exclaimed.

Alasdair frowned, glared in her direction, shook his head and, as if he thought that was not enough, raised his right hand. Melissa grimaced and fell silent. She could take the hint but was itching to pursue this line of enquiry.

'Greenwood, his details.' It was Alasdair's turn to be terse.

'Well, he came over at the very beginning of the war as a refugee. Volunteered to fight but was transferred to the security services due to his excellent languages. Much like you yourself, Alasdair. What are you thinking?'

'Well, did his credentials check out? It would not be difficult to pass off some Germans as Belgians.'

'He has family here in England. Of course, he was put on very junior, low-level stuff. But he has been with us for eight years. He is competent, not too flash, you know, and has risen through the ranks. I have had no reason to doubt him. Thus far.'

Something in his voice must have alerted Alasdair. 'Why now?'

'Someone has to be passing on stuff. I have whittled it down. So I promoted him to keep a weather eye on him.'

'Feeding false information?'

'Yes, a bit, but he has not appeared to put a step wrong. Thus far.'

'Do you think he could be in cahoots with the Countess's companion?'

At last, thought Melissa. She leant forward and then regretted it as the fug of Maundeville's cigarette hit her. There was already a full ashtray in front of him. She itched to open a window to let in some fresh air, or at least to empty the ashtray in the fire. She wondered if she would be breaching some servant protocol if she did so.

'He possibly might be.' Maundeville was caution itself.

'And Bernard Lyon. Where does he come in?'

'Your instincts are still razor sharp.' Maundeville gave a small grunt in acknowledgement. 'You are quite right. Special Branch have had their eye on him for quite some time.'

'And his gate-crashing of this weekend?'

'Yes, interesting that, ain't it?'

'His road accident?'

Maundeville tutted. 'Nothing escapes you, does it? All right, that was Colonel Manders. We had hoped to discourage him. Especially as Lyon was motoring down alone. Something must have been up for him to abandon his comforts. Normally he is chauffeur-driven door-to-door. It raised the alarm.'

'What went wrong?'

'Lyon must have driven hell for leather. Manders got him off the road by staging the accident, but he was too near here to turn him back.'

'Or too keen to be here,' Melissa interjected. What on earth could have possessed him to walk all that way in the rain? Looked at objectively, it was absurd.

'He was like a drowned rat when he got here.' Maundeville chuckled, as if picking up on her thoughts.

'You know Emma worked for the refugee charity he was involved with?'

'Yes, but ...' Alasdair raised his eyebrows but was silent.

'Oh, very well. Godfrey was very convincing that this seemed to be a domestic murder.'

'Deflecting away from a mole, then.'

'Yes.'

'So if you turn it on its head, leave Godfrey out, leave the family angle out, what have you got and what information do you now need?'

'Clearly we are going to have to go over that charity with a fine-tooth comb. It has some very aristocratic and influential people on the board and as trustees, though. That is why we had been going softly, softly with it. Thus far.'

'More fluffy aristos?' Melissa's voice was wry.

'Yes, but even you cannot be unaware of the fact that your title and connections open doors.'

'True, but I try not to use them!' She was full of indignation. How dare he suggest that she used influence? It went against all of her principles. How were they ever going to get a fairer world with behaviour like that?

'How can you ever know, though?' Maundeville asked. 'Just because things are not mentioned does not mean they are not considered by others and influence them accordingly.'

She had never considered this before. The fluffy aristo epithet had stung. But what if it was true? Did she appear just an upper-class twit? All her former work with the slum charities, work that she had to give up when Alasdair was home ... had that been just a token gesture? Had they secretly been laughing at her? The granddaughter of an earl who could never understand. She supposed the accent didn't help, but if she changed her accent, then who would she be?

'So what do you want us to do?' she asked.

'Melissa, your new friend will be Agnés Baume. Find out all you can about her and the Countess, any small detail might be useful. Alasdair, persuade Brigadier Ferguson to give his family handouts now. That should stop any ideas of murder from that quarter. He has been a damn fool. Although, if any other members of your family, Melissa, are thinking of blackmail, perhaps they have now been put off.'

'Oh, you knew?'

'Guessed. Bit off more than they could chew, didn't they? Though I suspect Emma supplied the information and George thought he could bank it. If he survives this blow to the head, how he will live with himself? I don't know.'

'He could hardly have thought he had stumbled on a spy ring. Not now after the war. That is what we are talking about, isn't it?'

'Yes,' Maundeville said. 'All eyes are on the Bolsheviks, but the Weimar Republic needs heavy scrutiny as well. We ignore Germany at our peril. We may have peace, but heaven knows what dissidents are flowing into this country as refugees. Special Branch has its hands full.'

Melissa took out her notebook from her crocodile clutch bag, opened it and pulled out the silver propelling pencil. 'So, here we are, I am ready. Let me get this straight. You have given up the idea that this is a member of the family bumping off the others to inherit?'

'Well, I toyed with the idea when Emma was murdered. We still have to link her, the charity and Bernard Lyon for definite, but it makes more sense that she knew something and was killed for that.'

'Then poor Meg, who heard a conversation about Germans. Oh, you realise she told Aunt Honor about it, but Honor was not listening? If the murderer finds out, will she not be in frightful danger?'

'You have warned her?'

'Oh yes, but she—'

'Don't you worry, my dear, that woman has a backbone of steel.'

'So, with George in hospital, do you think the murderer has stopped now?' Melissa asked.

'Depends how safe he or she feels.'

'So who do we think it is? Bernard Lyon?'

'A possible,' said Maundeville. 'Not the usual type to get his hands dirty, though, but I imagine if backed into a corner, like a rat, he might turn and fight.'

'The Countess?'

'A distinct possibility, but again I would have thought she might get someone else to do her dirty work.'

'There have been plenty of female assassins.'

'Usually in novels or domestic situations. Wives stabbing their husbands and so forth.'

'So she could have done it.'

'The doctor says so, but I am not sure.'

'Greenwood?' Alasdair asked.

'Possible, but what could be his motive? Unless you think your cousin had unmasked a spy ring, knew Greenwood was part of it and kept quiet about it. Rather unlikely, don't you think?'

'So, what was it she found out and told George that has him, in his turn, lying at death's door?'

'Oh Lord, now I have it.' Alasdair expelled his breath in a long sigh.

'What?' Melissa stared at him.

'There is something rather queer here, isn't there?'

TWENTY-NINE

'What on earth do you mean?' Melissa sounded genuinely confused.

Alasdair sighed. 'Men, darling.'

'Ye-e-e-s? Men what?'

'Men who like men. You know, men.' Alasdair coughed and inclined his head; she surely couldn't be that naïve.

'Homosexuals.' Maundeville was clearly tired of this shilly-shallying. 'You should be back on the payroll. Is there nothing you have missed?' His terse mood dispelled, his voice now carried approval and approbation.

'Well, it was just that I could not think what George could have picked up that was worth blackmailing for.' Alasdair could not help basking in a little of the glory. He needed just this recognition to lift his mood. He really was tired of the mire. It was time to move on. Could he do it? He had to.

Melissa removed the hand that she had automatically clasped over her mouth at the revelation. 'But who?'

'Well, we had our eye on the vicar for a while. Bit fey, that one.'

'Well, really, the vicar. How could you? But, who then?

Oh.' She gasped. 'Bernard Lyon?'

'Could be, but if he is, he is discreet. Special Branch have not picked up anything so far. In fact, they have picked up nothing in that direction at all.'

'Then how?' Melissa sounded confused.

Alasdair realised that she had missed it, in more ways than one. 'Arthur Baggeley told you?' he ventured.

'No, Henry Blake,' Maundeville replied.

'What, and missed his scoop?'

'Alasdair, he works for The Times not the Daily Mail,' Maundeville commented drily.

'So are you saying that someone is going around murdering people to stop anyone finding out they are homosexual?' Melissa was catching up. 'But we are in the 1920s! It is hardly Oscar Wilde.'

'Yes, well, what may be acceptable in some quarters is still illegal.'

'And susceptible to blackmail.' Alasdair finished.

'Yes, George went on a fishing expedition and made an unsavoury comment after we left the room. No, don't ask me to repeat it, but I believe it was that comment that alerted the murderer.'

'But if it was that comment made after dinner, then Bernard Lyon was not there, was he? Didn't he have food on a tray in his room and missed dinner all together?'

'That is true, but there was plenty of time for someone to tell him before Emma was killed.'

'But then Meg was talking about overhearing a conversation about Germans or Germany, Aunt Honor said.'

'But, and it is a big but, when it comes down to it,

all this is hearsay and speculation. Special Branch can hardly arrest anyone on this evidence. We have nothing, no concrete evidence whatsoever.'

'So, let us at least work on a timeline. Where are the reports of the interviews?' asked Alasdair. Melissa fetched them. 'Now draw a line horizontally from one side of the blackboard to the other.' He heard the chalk scrape the board. 'OK, mark that E for Emma. Another one further down M for Meg. Got it? And another G for George. OK, so let's fill it in. The screaming started, say three thirty, so that's the end of the timeline, right? So where do we begin?'

'What time did everyone go to bed?' Melissa asked.

'But this is useless,' barked Maundeville. They will all say they were tucked up in bed – leave it, we can do this timeline with Greenwood later.'

'But if you don't trust him, what's the point?'

'Oh, there is always a point,' Maundeville replied.

'So, what about the missing knife?' They had to do something. Alasdair couldn't believe that the man who had led the Secret Intelligence Service was being this wishy-washy. Throughout the war, the impression he had given was of being a decisive man of action and damn the consequences. Was that it? Was Melissa's family, his family, collateral damage? Was Maundeville that calculating? Of course he was.

'A search, you mean?' Maundeville asked. 'That would cause chaos.'

'You could do it over lunch while most people are in the dining room.' He had to influence him or the killing would not stop. He absolutely refused to accept any further deaths in the family or in this house. The house he had practically decided – no had decided – to make his future home. He would not have this dream, his beloved Melissa's dream, soured. Could you ever settle in a house that had seen these deaths? He clasped Melissa's hand and squeezed it. She squeezed back.

'True. I'll consider it.'

'So have you interviewed everyone now?'

'Yes, and we have nothing. Not on the spy, nor on the murderer. Or even enough to speculate circumstantially if they are one and the same.'

'Can we eliminate anyone?'

'The servants, Arthur Baggeley, Lady Honor and Brigadier Ferguson, you two, myself, but the rest?'

'So what now?'

'Alasdair, you missed out on some of the interviews. Godfrey has transcribed them. I want to go through them with you. I want you to see if there is anything I may have missed. You have always had a fine mind for dealing with detail, for dotting "i"s and crossing "t"s. We can do your damned timeline as well! And yes, Melissa my dear, you go check out the family.'

It was an order, but she was not ready yet. There was silence for a few moments; the fire crackled and Melissa listened to the rustling of the papers as Maundeville sifted through the files. There was something nagging at her. She looked out of the window. The thin sunlight had lost the battle for the morning and heavy dark clouds were rolling in.

'You know George implied that Emma had been seeing Bernard Lyon. That she had hopes in that direction and then she had changed. Described him as a vile sewer rat. I assumed that was because he was a blood-sucking banker, but what if she found out he was one of those men? Would he kill to protect himself? Oh, no. I have just worked out what the Countess was on about at dinner last night. What an idiot I have been.' She felt herself flushing and raised her hands to her hot cheeks.

''Fraid so, darling. Well, not the idiot bit,' Alasdair added quickly as he heard the squeak of indignation from his right.

'The utter …' Melissa spluttered, swallowed what she wanted to say and muttered, 'Cow. She was playing with me, with my ignorance. Is that what they did with Emma?'

'Perhaps. She could have been a smokescreen for his predilections. One who became too knowledgeable for their convenience.'

'Their?'

'Oh, I think we can safely say that the Countess and Bernard Lyon are in this together,' Alasdair replied. 'Don't you, Maundeville?'

'Yes, I have to agree, but how do we prove it?'

THIRTY

Melissa left Maundeville and Alasdair in the library. She glanced at her wristlet watch. It was approaching eleven o'clock. The others should be returning from church any moment now. She climbed the first flight of stairs and positioned herself by the huge Georgian-style window so she could watch for them returning.

Within five minutes, she should be able to see them coming up the drive. Five minutes during which she wished she had fetched a thicker cardigan, as the cold from the landing seemed to seep into her bones. She shivered and then saw the first of the group returning. They were bunched up together, almost as if they needed the comfort of the group, and yet at the same time they managed to convey to Melissa's watching eyes that they were apart – there was no cohesion, just pockets of rapport within the group. Melissa was glad she had chosen this vantage point as she was able to stare unashamedly and without being observed herself.

Brigadier Ferguson and Lady Honor led the group. Brigadier Ferguson had a stick, the first time that Melissa had seen him succumb to this outward sign of frailty and aging. Lady Honor was walking beside him, her arm looped through his. It gave the impression that she was almost holding him up. Melissa smiled. The power behind the throne. Today, Lady Honor wore a nearly full-length tweed coat with a long fur collar and a huge hat. Clothes from another age. Imperious, reiterating her status to the community. She would have been instantly identifiable in the front pew. Perhaps hoping to declare all was still well with the world. But was it? Melissa thought disconsolately. Would this house ever be released from the stain of the blood that had spilled here? She recalled the image of Meg stabbed to death in the boot room. Once seen, could it be unseen? If they decided to live here, she would have that room dismantled and decorated. She could almost smell that rich tang of blood again. Was this what Alasdair suffered but on a grander scale? Grander? Hardly, a descent into hell more like. How could he have hidden this from her? But how, until now, would she have had any inkling of just what he might be going through? Blood and death.

She returned her attention to the path below her. Henry Blake and Lottie came next. She too had her arm looped through his, but in contrast she positively strummed with vibrancy, her steps short and quick, her face alight with some enthusiasm. Lottie was so exuberant, so alive. Melissa wondered what it would take to dim that light. Yet that spark of vitality was a contrast to the sombre dark blue drop-waisted coat that encased her, her blonde curls bound by the matching cloche hat.

Henry Blake, in his turn, appeared distracted. His face was in the shadow of a wide-brimmed hat; beneath the brim, he was frowning as if in deep concentration. Even from this distance, Melissa could see the furrows between his eyes disappearing up into the hat. He had on a dark grey, long, loose, duster-style raincoat. The grey man, blending naturally into the background. Melissa was impressed that Lottie had managed to get him to church. She wouldn't have thought him the type. Certainly not for their quaint country church and their young, callow vicar. Perhaps he had been concentrating on his copy?

Behind them, with a pronounced gap both in front and behind, was the Honourable Rose Tennant. Surprisingly, she was on her own. She had made an effort, dressed in a fashionable violet drop-waisted coat with darker velvet lapels; this was picked up in the wide-brimmed hat and dark purple leather shoes and handbag. But it was her face that arrested Melissa. It was ugly with emotion. Not grief, Melissa decided, not pain, but anger – her whole posture demonstrated temper, something dark and brooding. Melissa shivered. She must get a cardigan, or at least buy some stouter underwear to protect against the cold.

So preoccupied was she that she almost missed observing the Countess and Bernard Lyon. They went to church? But surely the Countess must be Roman Catholic. Resplendent in furs, and with no concession to an English Sunday morning, there was a slash of bright red lipstick as she inclined her head to listen to whatever it was Bernard Lyon was telling her. There was some distance between them and Rose, so there would be little point in asking Rose later if she had overheard anything. Rose seemed so caught up in her black cloud that Melissa doubted she would be much use as a witness anyway. She wondered idly if she ought to take up lip-reading. Could one be successful from this distance?

And then her jaw dropped and much became clear – the last stragglers of the group came into view. It was Arthur Baggeley and, smiling up at him prettily, her face transformed by mischief – and was it flirtation? – was Agnés Baume. Even allowing for her rather shabby, ill-fitting and unbecoming dark coat, sensible black shoes and handbag, for that moment there was an arresting elfin beauty about her. Melissa grinned. Now here was someone she could take in hand. She did so much like organising.

She leant over the banister and watched Smithers open the front door. So, Sunday morning church did not extend to the servants. She wondered idly if they were given any option.

Lady Honor and Brigadier Ferguson came in first, leading the gaggle of guests, shedding their coats as they made for coffee in the morning room. Melissa turned and began to make her way down the stairs but had to halt to make way for Rose, who still appeared to be in a frightful temper. She marched past Melissa, taking the stairs two at a time. Her mother would have been appalled at the lack of ladylike characteristics; all that sport seemed to be having an effect.

Melissa drifted into the morning room, a large open room at the back of the house under the guest wing. It had French windows out onto the patio that ran most of the length of the rear of the house. The views down the lawns and over into the wooded New Forest were superb, especially now the leaves were turning, vibrant with the colours of autumn. The room was decorated in a pale discreet green, the ubiquitous chintz-covered sofas picking up the green and adding large pink peony blooms. It all cried out somewhat faded taste and money. Looking at all the tables and mantelpieces covered in knick-knacks, Melissa again wondered about the servants and dusting.

There was no sign of Maundeville or Alasdair. Lottie and Henry were sitting on a sofa facing the garden, so on a whim she decided to join them. Lady Honor was wielding the coffee pot from the silver salver, quite expertly, and she handed Melissa a cup as she passed. Melissa smiled as the door opened and Smithers bustled in to take over coffee duties, his face portraying disapproval – perhaps Her Ladyship was not meant to serve coffee. Melissa could hear the crackle of the fire in the beautiful sandstone fireplace. She caught the scent of pine and watched the blue sparks as the logs burned. It was then that she realised the significance. Everyone in the room was talking quietly, as subdued and discreet as the furnishings.

Henry and Lottie appeared very sombre. Lottie's former vitality had dissipated; up close, her eyes were red-rimmed with dark circles beneath

'How was church?' Melissa opened with.

'Love, forgiveness and healing,' Henry replied sourly. 'How are you getting on with your sleuthing?'

'Oh, it's hardly that,' Melissa countered. 'What about you two? Any insights?'

'Yes, I damn well have.' Henry lowered his voice. 'This investigation is all wrong. They have missed the most basic of police techniques.'

'What do you mean?'

'Look, I may not have fought in the war, but driving

an ambulance gave me a very clear idea of wounds, combat and death. Something I had hoped to forget.' He squeezed Lottie's knee. 'As did Lottie here. She saw more than her fair share too. Seeing George like that and taking him to the hospital has just brought it all back for both of us. You see, to kill Emma and the maid in such a way that they did not fight back required cunning, skill and utter ruthlessness. Usually death is messy. And that is another thing. If you had stabbed someone, you would be covered in blood. Why have the police not conducted even a rudimentary search of our rooms to see if there are any bloodstains on our clothing?'

'Well, I guess they have been preoccupied.'

'Oh come on. It is now Sunday, nearly two days since the first murder. It is either ·pure incompetence or they think they know who the murderer is and are just focused on that.'

It was a little too close to the mark for Melissa. Mindful of Maundeville's investigation, she attempted to divert the conversation. 'But how do you know so much about the police?'

'I am a reporter. I spent some time going out with them on my patch in the East End and the docks. The sailors and lascars are frequently getting into scraps, and the knife is the weapon of choice. I have seen my fair share of knifed victims, and as I said before, it is messy. Lots of blood. So what is going on here? It is either something underhand or sheer incompetence. I tell you, I am not letting Lottie out of my sight. Who would have thought it?' They smiled a little shyly at each other, clearly unafraid to show that they were besotted with each other, before he added, 'And you and Alasdair had better watch your backs.'

'Why us in particular?'

'Oh come on, Mellie. I may be an investigative reporter but even the most stupid person here must have worked out by now that you two are up to your eyes in it.'

'No, don't be silly.' Melissa was beginning to panic; he was so near to the truth, and he was frightening her. She looked at Lottie and saw that her own fear was reflected back in her eyes.

'Very well,' he said. 'Have it your way, but heed my warning – humans are animals underneath that sophisticated veneer. During the war, we experienced ambulance convoys strafed by the enemy planes, hospitals hit by allegedly stray mortar shells, men screaming in pain for the lack of painkillers, and kind, gentle country doctors turned into butchers.' He was silent for a few moments but then gestured to the room. 'Remember, a cornered animal is a very dangerous animal indeed.'

THIRTY-ONE

Privately, Melissa had to agree with Henry, but of course he knew nothing about the spy issue, although she strongly suspected he knew more than he was letting on. If Maundeville was correct, then she could happily dismiss her family from any involvement in the murders, despite the fact that one was dead and another was at death's door. She looked out the window. Any warmth or beauty seemed to have been leached out of the day. Even the popping of the flames in the fire seemed to presage danger, as though they echoed the gunfire that Henry had talked about. Were she and Alasdair fools to be caught up in this? Would it not be better to hide beneath the parapet until Maundeville had done his work?

She sighed, but Maundeville had tasked her with getting closer to Agnés Baume. She glanced across the room. Agnés was standing by the fireplace, her cheeks rosy from the heat of the fire, still close in conversation with Arthur Baggeley. Melissa moved closer. They seemed to be making plans for the afternoon. If so, she would have to make sure that she sat with her at luncheon. She needed to find out about their plans and to get herself involved. She noticed the Countess was also watching the scene, her jaw working, lending a spiteful nuance to her features. Perhaps now was the time to put a spoke in the Countess's wheel.

Melissa dodged around a small table and walked up to the Countess, effectively blocking Agnés from her view. Melissa sensed her irritation, but when the Countess turned her reptilian gaze upon her, those features were bland and apparently open. Melissa was reminded of the lizards in London Zoo with their nictitating third eyelid. One blink vitriol, one blink bland? She smiled, apparently genuinely, at the Countess. 'I am so pleased to have this chance for a chat. We have hardly met this weekend what with everything going on. Ghastly, isn't it?'

'Quite. When I came to the countryside, I expected hunting, shooting, fun games. Even perhaps a little game of murder after dinner. You have played it? But real murder, people dying. Never, never.' The Countess shivered theatrically, but her eyes were sparkling. 'You seem to have shed your husband. It must be quite a burden for you. Not quite what you imagined when you married the dashing soldier, n'est pas?'

Oh no you don't, thought Melissa. 'Indeed, but for you, coming from France, there must have been huge upheaval. Do you live in England now?'

'Yes, like you, I have a small service flat in London. The countryside is only bearable according to the comfort of the house. Here, it is good, at least it is warm and the plumbing works. Some of the houses are horrible. But what can one do? It is usually fun to come to these weekends and see the English in all their glory.'

Melissa did not think this was a compliment, and come

to think of it, how did she know they had a service flat in London? She was sure neither she or Alasdair had spoken to her at any length. Had she been doing her homework on them and was showing off her knowledge? What could possibly be her motive? They were small fry, and surely they had only been recruited on the spot once Emma had been killed? Perhaps she did her homework on all the members of a house party before she came. If so, and if she was not a spy, what was the point? Was she a blackmailer too? A picker-up of dropped, indiscreet trifles?

'Do you think you will stay here?' the Countess continued. 'Will the country life suit you? For me it would be absolutely dire, so dull. Once the guests have gone, what is there to do?'

Melissa had been momentarily startled by the Countess's in-depth knowledge of her and Alasdair's affairs, as she had no doubt intended, but Melissa was made of sterner stuff. This was almost a declaration of war, and nothing was going to distract her from her prey. She tried again. 'Have you never lived in the country?'

The Countess narrowed her eyes. 'Yes, my husband has estates in France. He liked it there, but me, no, only during the summer when Paris is empty and boring, and even then I would prefer to be on the Riviera. I am lucky I have so many friends.'

'Oh, you are married? Does your husband not travel with you?'

'No, he prefers his estates. The land of his ancestors.'

'Oh, where are they? Would I know them?' Keep going, she thought. The Countess must divulge something eventually, if only out of politeness. No wonder Maundeville had got nowhere. She was a master of prevarication and riposte. Clearly, this woman had something to hide, but how on earth could they hope to wear her down to the truth?

'I think not. It is not such a great estate. Not like Versailles.'

'Is it near Versailles?' Gosh, this was like pulling teeth, thought Melissa.

'No, it is near where the fighting was, close to the border of Belgium and Germany. Not a good place to be. As I told your dear Maundeville, my pauvre husband is missing. I have no idea where he might be.' She dramatically searched about her, and then Bernard Lyon leant over with a pristine white handkerchief. Melissa caught the look of wry amusement on his face before it was replaced, not quite quickly enough, by one of polite concern. 'Oh, Bernard, you are so kind. I am so upset, so afraid.' She clutched his arm and allowed herself to be led away.

Melissa almost ground her teeth in frustration. Would she never get an opportunity to delve further? She did hope Maundeville had been more successful. At that moment, the vicar arrived. He accepted his coffee and moved towards her, Melissa glanced around the room; the only people missing were Brigadier Ferguson and Rose. Brigadier Ferguson she could understand, but Rose, where was she? Did she not realise it was unsafe to be alone, or had she locked herself in her room for safety? Still, she could not worry about her now. She had her mission from Maundeville,

She moved towards the fireplace, smiling to the vicar in encouragement so that he followed along. 'So sorry I missed the service, Vicar, I was having the third degree over this unpleasantness.'

'No more incidents, I hope?' His voice was full of concern. Melissa shook her head in reply. 'Perhaps this has been the end of it. I caught Brigadier Ferguson just as I was coming in. I have advised him to clear the air and make his intentions clear. This idea of his of testing the family is definitely not a good idea in my opinion.'

'So you firmly believe it was one of the family?' Melissa was incredulous.

'Well.' The vicar coughed. 'I would not put it quite like that, but you must see ...'

'What ho, Vicar. Putting your foot in it, Harold?' Arthur Baggeley slapped the vicar heartily on the back, nearly sending him flying. He frowned at Melissa and made a grimace over his shoulder, unseen by the vicar, as if to say don't bait the natives.

Melissa gave a small, resigned moue in return. There really were too many cooks on the guest list. Did they all fancy themselves as detectives?

'Shame you missed church, Melissa,' he said. 'Good sermon, Harold. Have you met Agnés?' He said it with a soft, rolling attempt at French pronunciation, and Melissa knew for sure in that moment that he was smitten. She just hoped Agnés was not a murderer or a spy, otherwise he was destined to more unhappiness. 'Thought I'd take Agnés over to my place after lunch, give her a bit of a break. She can't dance attendance on the Countess all the time, eh?'

'Indeed.' Definitely smitten, on the way to courting. Flash, the family pile. I may be a little long in the tooth but look at my estate. She then felt awful to be so cynical. Arthur really was a very nice man.

'Say, how about you come with us?'

Melissa glanced at Agnés, who flushed prettily. Dear Arthur, he was so old-fashioned – a chaperone. It was almost like declaring his intentions here and now. Before she could take up the opportunity, the vicar assented enthusiastically. Blow that, Melissa thought. 'Well, if I can give my husband the slip once again, perhaps I can manage to come along too.'

If the vicar was set on ruining their tête-à-tête, she too could play with fire. Then she might as well use it to cosy up to Agnés and see if she could gain some insights. Agnés smiled at her, and looking into her open, fresh face, apparently devoid of any artifice, Melissa realised this could be a tall order or a wild goose chase.

Brigadier Ferguson came in. He looked flustered, his face in high colour. 'Look, chaps, I want to have a family meeting after luncheon. Shall we say back in here? Honor is going to offer some bridge in the drawing room for any other guests that wish to play. Maundeville is continuing to do his thing, of course. He still says we must all remain here. So we might as well try and make the best of it.'

'Oh, do you think we will be allowed to pop over to your estate, Arthur?'

'Can't see why not. It is just a short walk over the fields. Not much further than the village this morning. And there has to be safety in numbers, what?'

THIRTY-TWO

Alasdair had rather a tedious morning. It was clear that Maundeville had been thorough. He could find no fault with his line of questioning, and unfortunately could find no chinks in the armour of the answers gained from the guests and potential suspects. Every reply seemed reasonable. Alibis, on the whole, were unable to be substantiated, or if they were, they were unreliable. Maundeville had been right; the timeline had not been revealing. It had resulted in a thorough overhaul of the interviews; however, he could see no way of breaking the impasse that Maundeville found himself in and eliminate any of the guests. It appeared from Maundeville's notes that anyone or no one could have committed the murders. Alasdair thumped the arm of his chair in frustration.

Colonel Manders was not present at the time of the murders so he was eliminated. The same could be said of Arthur Baggeley and Harold James, the vicar, as they had returned home after dinner. Of course, there was an outside chance that they could have returned. Alasdair wondered how well the house was locked up at night. Henry Blake came out of his room when the screaming started; he thought he'd seen Godfrey Greenwood but could not swear to it, as his journalistic antenna were concentrated on the drama below. Godfrey Greenwood also claimed not to be able to identify any of his fellow guests – and so it went on. Even the family seemed unable to commit themselves. It was all very unsatisfactory. If any of them were in cahoots, they certainly were not providing each other with alibis. What was the saying? Only the guilty had alibis. In which case, who was it?

As to the time of Meg's murder, a murder that took place practically under the noses of the kitchen staff and not forgetting the constable … All he could say was the murderer of Meg was not himself, Maundeville, the Countess or Godfrey Greenwood, as they had all been in the library at the time.

George's attempted murder was even more of a fug, with some of the women in one place and some of the men in another, but once again no one appeared able to account for one another's movements. Alasdair blamed Brigadier Ferguson's generosity with the cocktails, wine at dinner and the port and liqueurs. The whole thing was a right mess. His opinion was that it was going to take painstaking police work by the experts to unravel it. He sighed. 'You are going to instigate a search of the bedrooms, aren't you?' He turned his attention to Maundeville. This should have been done right at the beginning. It was too late now to consider the guests' sensitivities.

'Yes, damn nuisance you can't see. I could have done with your eyes.'

'Huh, so could I,' retorted Alasdair drily.

'Sorry, old chap, but you know what I mean. I would

use Godfrey, but then I would have to watch him and the search would take forever.'

'Look, I hate to say this, but why don't you call in Special Branch now? They have the manpower. Or at least recall Colonel Manders. You need help. This is a large house to cover. Also, you have three possible murders on your hands now, and I can't see that we are any closer to solving it, or to unmasking your spy.'

'OK, I agree with you. I just hate to admit defeat. I'll get Colonel Manders back down. If he drives like the wind, he can be here mid-afternoon. I'll call Special Branch and take advice. I think you are right; the Countess is far too canny to fold. It was probably naïve of me to think she would. I was just clutching at straws, but I am getting desperate. We have to stop the leak.'

'So will you wait to do the room search until Manders gets here?'

'Yes, that seems sensible. He, I and, hopefully, your wife can conduct the search later. Special Branch may even be here by then.'

'I must say, I will be relieved. This whole thing has got totally out of hand. Are you sure you can find nothing on Greenwood?'

'If there is anything, we cannot find it. He has covered his tracks well. If we could find some link between him and the Countess, well then ... But during the interviews there was not a hint that they knew each other. The only tenuous link was that her companion is Belgian, the same as Greenwood.'

'But she is aristocracy. Did you know? Was he? Would they have even moved in the same circles?'

Vicki Goldie

'I said it was tenuous.' Maundeville sounded beaten. 'Do you know, Alasdair, my boy, I think it is time I retired. Moved to the country. Grew cabbages.' The sigh was long and low. 'What was that racket?' He looked at his fob watch. 'The damn gong. Good Gad, it's luncheon already. Another morning gone. I'll go fetch your wife. I could do with stretching my legs.'

A short time later, Melissa popped her head around the door of the library, spied Alasdair and escorted him back to their room, despite his complaints about being late for lunch.

'I need to have a quick chat, Alasdair. The Brigadier has called a family powwow after lunch, but I have been invited to accompany Harold and Agnés to Arthur's estates. I think he wants a chaperone. Isn't that sweet? Can you go to the family meeting and I'll tail Agnés?'

'Sweet, maybe, but dangerous. She could be our murderess.'

'Could she?'

'Well, one of them has to be.' Alasdair flopped back on the bed. 'God, I am tired. I feel so useless. You know, Maundeville as good as told me. What can I do? What was I thinking? That I, a blind man, could hold my own in society? Work again even?'

Eggshells. Eggshells. 'Oh Alasdair, of course you are not useless. Would Brigadier Ferguson be considering offering us all this if you were useless?' What would it take to make him realise that he could have a full and active life. Perhaps not the one he had been destined, for but a different one. A new challenge.

'That could just be charity and you know it.'

'Charity? Don't be absurd. Someone has to run this place and get it in order. Why not you, us?' Sometimes it was hard, even for her, to keep up this constant jolly hockey sticks front. Sometimes she would like to be grumpy, sad, petulant or just have a cry.

There was silence. Melissa sighed. She didn't care; he would just have to lump it. 'Do you want lunch?'

'No.' He turned his head away from her voice. 'I am suddenly not hungry. I think I'll sleep.'

Melissa checked her hair, applied a small splash of lipstick and tiptoed out of the room, making sure the key was in the lock should Alasdair want to use it. Outside the door, she took a deep breath, lowered her shoulders, raised her chest. I am the granddaughter of an earl, she told herself repeatedly as she walked along the upstairs landing and down the staircase with all the determination she could muster.

Entering the dining room, she noted that the heated silver chafing dishes were out. Clearly, the staffing was minimal again, and poor Smithers was still on duty. There was a lovely thick vegetable soup, pork cutlets, apple sauce, green beans, carrots and mashed potato. With a pang, Melissa realised that Alasdair would have loved this spread, but he had chosen his bed and must lie on it, literally. And she should leave him to wallow; she could do no more when he was in one of his black moods. As chance would have it, there was a space next to Arthur, and she plonked herself next to him. 'I say, Arthur.' She tapped his arm quite firmly to attract his attention away from Agnés for a moment. 'I have to go to a family meeting just after lunch. Are you able to wait a short while and then I can accompany you this afternoon?'

Arthur looked at Agnés. She could see he was torn. 'Well, Harold offered to come, but I see, no, we will wait for you. I'll let him know.' He leaned closer. 'Confidentially, I don't want her tied up by Countess Spiteful and ruining the afternoon.'

'Well, they should be playing cards, but I take your point. Why don't you use the pink snug and I'll find you as soon as I can? I love the sobriquet. Countess Spiteful – suits her.' She smiled.

'Where is Alasdair?'

Her smile faded. 'He has a headache and is having a rest.' The tone of her voice brooked no further enquiries. Arthur turned his attention back to Agnés. Thus free to scope the room, Melissa noted that Rose was sitting with Henry and Lottie, which was a relief. One less person to worry about. She still seemed out of sorts, but then, if your prospective fiancée was lying at death's door, you would hardly be dancing the fandango. Melissa turned her attention to her food. She picked at it; delicious as it was, her stomach was rebelling. The tension of the last few days was playing havoc with her appetite. She glanced up and saw that Honor was watching her, a small frown on her face. She gave a quick smile down the table and forced some more food into her mouth. She should not waste it. They were so lucky to have enough when many were starving. She continued to pick away at it until a passable space appeared on the plate and Smithers whisked it away. Foregoing pudding, she made her way into the morning room to await the family meeting with the Brigadier.

It was a sorry bunch that met after lunch. Melissa had

left Alasdair to sleep and gave his apologies. There was, of course, no Emma and no George. Just Melissa, Lottie and Henry Blake, the latter two now seeming joined at the hip. She was glad; they were a nice couple, a couple who had come through adversity together. No matter that they seemed to live a rather fast life now. Perhaps if Brigadier Ferguson gave Lottie enough money, they could marry and maybe, just maybe, settle down. The Brigadier looked at them rather bewildered. He looked like a man who had had the stuffing knocked out of him.

'I hadn't intended this to happen,' he muttered. 'This weekend has been a disaster. Poor, poor Emma. There is no news on George, or they won't tell me.' He leant forward in the chair, a rather incongruous figure, this bear of a man in the small chintz seat. His shoulders began to shake. Melissa was horrified to realise that he was crying. 'Sometimes, I think this family is cursed.'

Melissa went over to him, knelt on the floor at his feet. 'No, Uncle,' she said gently, placing one hand on his knee. 'We are not cursed, just flamboyant, vivacious, enthusiastic and perhaps a tiny bit unlucky.' She couldn't bear to see this once great man, commander of troops and the agent of so much fun in the holidays of her youth, brought so low.

He pulled out an enormous cotton handkerchief and blew his nose. 'I cannot help feeling that if I hadn't arranged this weekend, this would never have happened.'

'But then what a boring life we would lead. Richard and Henry would never have wanted you to live a restrained life. Goodness me, you never did, and you absolutely can't start now.'

He cleared his throat. 'Very well, my dear, here is what

231

I propose to do. Charlotte, I will settle £2000 on you now with a further £2500 when you marry.'

'You can't do that,' Henry Blake spluttered and rose to his feet. 'You will have every cad and fortune-hunter in the country chasing her.'

'In that case, I suggest you get on with it and declare yourself. Take it from one who married up himself. Pride is not worth worrying about. It is what you do with your life that counts. Still, of course, she may not have you.' His watery eyes twinkled as he glanced at the pink-faced Lottie.

'George, should he survive, as my only nephew will get £5000, then he can start that motor business he is on about. Oh yes, I am not such an old duffer that I don't know what's happening in my own house. He can be an idiot, but he is my idiot, and I want to give him a chance.'

'Now, as for you.' He turned his gaze to Melissa, still sitting at his feet. 'You have a choice. You can have the same as your cousin Lottie, or you can stay here, with that husband of yours, and give running this estate a go. I will make you my heirs and one day this will all be yours. What do you say?'

THIRTY-THREE

As soon as he heard Mellie's footsteps recede. Alasdair kicked off his shoes, tiptoed over to the door and locked it. For good measure, he put the chair under the door, as they had overnight. He was exhausted. So many people, so many new rooms, steps to count, furniture to remember. How was he expected to cope? The place was vast. At St Dunstan's, they had used tactile maps made of thick card and string. He needed someone to make one for every area of the house and the estate. He felt a tic beginning in the outer corner of his left eye. He raised his hand to it to stop the movement. He may not be able to see, but his body still seemed to want him to be able to. The signals were there, frustrated and stressing. He moved back to the bed, removed his jacket, lay down and pulled the eiderdown over himself. He needed to think and he might as well be warm. He closed his eyes.

Awaking later, he checked his watch and cursed. He had slept for two hours. Still, he felt better, calmer and knew what he wanted to do, but how to achieve it? He was sure that Davies would help. He padded over to where he assumed the bell pull was. Yes, to the left of the fireplace was the old-fashioned pull. Hopefully, Thomas was in the servant's hall and would come to his aid. He was too dependent on Melissa. It was not fair. He was not fair. He had to do this his way.

He felt around for his shoes, unlaced them and put them on. Now for the jacket. Where had he flung it? He needed to be more organised, more independent. It would also help if he was less churlish. He had to stop feeling sorry for himself. Move on, as they said. Easier said than done. What he needed was a project, and this could be it. There was a rattling at the door, and then a knock.

'You needed me, sir?' It was Thomas. Alasdair made his way over to the door, unhooked the chair, unlocked the door and opened it.

'Can't be too careful, don't you know?' he muttered sheepishly.

'Of course, sir. Mrs Charters has gone off to Arthur Baggeley's estate. Do you wish to follow?'

Alasdair smiled; he knew his wife would have made plans and followed them. They made a good pair, and he was now determined to spoil her. She deserved it.

'No, Thomas, thank you. Have you seen Davies?'

'Yes, he was in the servants' hall for luncheon and was still there when I came up to answer your bell.'

'Good, oh, where have I left my jacket?'

'Here, sir.'

'Thank you. Very well, any way you could get me to Davies?'

'Why don't I accompany you to the estates office? And then I can fetch Davies.'

'Remind me where it is?'

'At the back of the house, at the end of the servants' wing.'

'Is it going to be a great palaver getting there?'

'No, we can go through one of the snugs and out of the French windows, and then across the garden.'

'Phew. I would have to rearrange this house if I am ever to find my way around alone.'

'Well, I think, sir, that it was designed like that so as the estate manager lived above the shop, so to speak.'

'Really? OK, so how many offices and snugs are there in the main house?

'Four, sir, not including the library.'

'Well there must be one I can use.'

'The Brigadier has one, Lady Honor has another, that leaves two others. One was used by the housekeeper, the other is a sort of small library. It is off the main library.'

'Jolly good, Thomas, well recced. Take me to the smaller library and let's see if that could suit.'

The minute Thomas opened the door and led him in, Alasdair could sense this was a smaller room from the echo of their footsteps.

'Sir, in this room, from here is twelve o'clock, large sash window to the garden; three o'clock, doors to the main library; nine o'clock, the fireplace. There is a writing desk in the far-right corner, at two o'clock. Two chairs in front of the fire. In the middle of the room is a small oval table with two dining chairs around it, but it has a bloody great floral arrangement in the middle. Some sort of dried thing.'

'Thanks for the heads up. Least this time we won't be hit by snipers. Just Lady Honor if I shatter her floral arrangements, what?'

'Blooming stupid, if you ask me.' Thomas sniffed. 'Every surface in this house is cluttered with something. Much better at the flat. Clean, tidy, no junk.'

Alasdair laughed. 'Don't let Lady Honor hear you say that about her knick-knacks. She'll have your guts for garters. But you are right, we could strip this and make it safe for me. Can you fetch Davies? Tell him I won't keep him long, I know it is a Sunday.'

'He may not be a servant, but I'll bet he is still working.' Then, perhaps seeing Alasdair's crestfallen face, he added, 'Well, I doubt there is much to do hereabouts. Hardly the great metropolis, is it, sir?'

Alasdair waited for the door to close. He then backed slowly to the doors. These came though from the great entrance hall, as most rooms seemed to. Placing his heels against the door, he turned left and then walked along the wall, feeling his way with the tips of his fingers. He counted the steps until he hit the wall at right angles. He had encountered fitted bookshelves. Turning, running his fingers along the shelves, he counted until he felt a wall again. He reached up, running his hand over the wall. Yes, here was the old-fashioned bell pull. He was cautious now, as he knew he must be close to the fireplace, which would have sharp corners and varying heights. He stopped when his outstretched right hand came in contact with what must be the fireplace. The mantle was at shoulder height, and, yes, the edge would have done some damage, especially if he had had his head down. Smooth wood with a sharp corner at each end.

Carefully, as forewarned by Thomas, he ran his hand along the edge of the mantle. Whenever his hand strayed further towards the back, he encountered something made of porcelain – breakable and no doubt valuable. At the end of the fireplace, there was more blank wall and then built-in bookcases, he assumed to match the other side. Damn, he had forgotten the number of paces. What was it? Ten paces to the fireplace, five for the fireplace and presumably another ten if the room was in proportion. He congratulated himself on not falling over the fireside chairs which Thomas had mentioned. Reaching the corner, he turned and began pacing the outside wall. He stumbled when his knee hit a low coffee table; he felt around and encountered two chairs. Thomas had not mentioned this table, but perhaps it had been obscured by the dried flower arrangement in the middle. He negotiated his way round the furniture, resting his fingers on the curtains, presumably for the sash window. Five paces and he was at the writing desk. Another wooden dining chair was pulled up in front of it. He pulled the chair out and sat down.

The desk was long and flat-topped, with what felt like a leather inlay. There was a desk drawer below on either side. The papers in the desk were useless to him, even if he has wanted to snoop – blindness. At the back of the desk was a letter rack, empty. Mercifully, the rest of the desktop appeared clear. He ran his palms over the smooth top, enjoying the tactile sensation of the almost warm, polished wood as it gave way to the leather. He wondered what colour the leather was. Red or the more traditional green? He then realised that his hands were dusty. Perhaps if they got rid of all the ornaments, someone would have time to dust properly. The door opened.

'Here he is, sir, Davies, I found him.'

'Come in, Davies, have a seat. Now, tell me, how are we going to make this estate pay its way then?'

THIRTY-FOUR

Melissa had caught up with Arthur and Agnés in the morning room. They had been sitting in seclusion, apparently engrossed in each other. They leapt apart when Melissa entered, Agnés colouring prettily.

'What ho. Time to be moving. Mrs Stokes will have the kettle on,' Arthur blustered. As they entered the hall, the vicar, Harold, was waiting ready, then Smithers appeared and immediately disappeared off to get their overcoats.

A short time later, well wrapped up against a chilly wind, they made their way down the drive past the cattle grid at the end. It had been agreed to go the long way round as neither the vicar nor Agnés had gumboots.

'What is that for?' asked Agnés, pointing at the grid.

'Animals are turned out to graze in the forest. They are all owned by someone, but they make a hell of a mess of a country garden if they get on your land. This contraption stops them getting in,' Arthur explained.

They went down the lane, littered with autumn leaves in all colours from the trees edging the road. It afforded an excellent view of the small village below them. Here and there, Melissa could see chimney smoke from those houses with inhabitants who could afford winter fuel during the day. To be sure, she thought, there would be foraging for forest wood, but that would be conserved for when winter really did begin to bite. Today the sun shone, it was crisp but not cold enough for a log fire in many of the households. Guiltily, she thought of the fires at Pennstone blazing in every grate, not to mention the work involved in maintaining them.

After a walk of about twenty minutes, the house and estates of Arthur Baggeley came into view. Agnés exclaimed in admiration and Melissa smiled. The reason for the longer walk became clear. Where Pennstone Manor was mainly built in Purbeck stone with higgledy-piggledy bits added on from different time periods, Arthur's house was pure Georgian, stark, simple and elegant. The sun shining on it lifted the austerity and gave it some warmth. Pennstone Manor was mostly hidden from the road, down its long and winding drive. However, this house stood out; it was meant to be viewed and admired, a statement of wealth and of taste.

They turned in past another cattle grid, and Melissa fell back a little, wanting to give Arthur and Agnés some privacy. It was Arthur's moment. She felt he deserved it. The vicar fell in with Melissa. 'I have been meaning to have a word with you,' he murmured. 'I have had something on my mind since George was attacked.'

'Come on, you two,' Arthur called. 'Don't dawdle, Mrs Stokes will have the tea on the go already.'

'Perhaps on the way back,' Melissa muttered as they sped up their pace to catch up their host.

The door was opened by Mr Stokes, the butler, another husband and wife combination, Melissa surmised. However, this wife, Mrs Stokes, was much younger, a round jolly country woman with a glorious Hampshire accent.

Mrs Stokes eyed up the guests; she smiled with approval at Melissa – Mrs Charters – in her tweed suit and sensible brogues. Here was someone ready for the countryside. If village rumour was true, she would do very well at Pennstone. Lady Honor needed the help. She turned her attention to the other young lady and sniffed. Foreign. Nice manners, though.

Melissa watched Agnés endearing herself to Mrs Stokes. Lawd, she must have had enough practice with the Countess. She nibbled a fish paste sandwich and eyed the cakes; they looked good. Mrs Stokes allowed Agnés to pour the tea into fragile bone china teacups from a hideous silver teapot. Amazing what ghastly heirlooms they all had. However, there was little evidence of that in this well-appointed room. It was simple and minimalist in a modern style. The ubiquitous chintz sofas were nowhere in sight. The room had dove-grey painted walls with darker accents around the windows and doors. The floor was dark wood parquet, polished to perfection. An elegant geometric rug in greys, black and cream lay in front of the fire, and another, larger one in the centre of the room. On it stood a low ebony table, upon which resided the yummy tea things. The chairs and two sofas were in a dove-grey leather. The whole room breathed elegance and restraint. The only extraneous decoration was a large mantle clock featuring Diana and her hounds hunting a stag and a huge Venetian mirror behind it. This was clearly an heirloom. It should have been incongruous, but its glorious ebullience was restrained and complemented by the clear lines of the rest of the room.

In utter contrast, Melissa realised, to her aunt's copious Victoriana household. Did her aunt still need all that stuff? It was nice to have a few statement pieces from the past, but it looked like Honor was clinging to the past ad infinitum. Was that what happened when you lost your children? An incapacity to dispose of anything that they may have touched, even if it was hideous?

She wondered what Arthur had done with all the former clutter, the hunting pictures, the bonbon dishes, the Spode. This was a room that Alasdair would admire, she realised. Clean, neat, nothing extraneous to knock over. Everything was utilitarian but somehow stylish. It forced her to view Arthur Baggeley in a different light. In this room, there was absolutely no reflection of his former wife. It was as if by expunging her from the décor, he could cut out the pain and become a modern man, fresh, born anew. Perhaps this was what Aunt Honor had to learn, but how to teach her? Maybe they could just clear a few rooms to start with. She could give the reason as Alasdair – say he might break something precious. Or was that beyond the pale? It was true, but playing on his disability to her own advantage seemed wrong somehow.

It was also blissfully warm. As part of his renovation, Arthur had also clearly introduced modern central heating. She had missed the large cast iron radiators about the room at first, as they had been painted to match the walls, but goodness, she could feel their value in their heat. He must have some very powerful boilers to produce this temperature. Gosh, with heating like this, they would not need all the fires in every room at Pennstone. Forget the knick-knacks; she would investigate the cost of proper heating. Arthur, of course, would be able to recommend someone. She just hoped it was not a crippling price, but then she remembered that Brigadier Ferguson was rich and so it could count as an investment in the estate. Pleased with her calculations, she tuned back into the tea.

The tea was hot and delicious with just the right amount of milk. There were even scones, cream and bright red strawberry jam. 'How lovely. Thank you so much, Arthur, this is a real treat away from the mayhem at the Manor. How are you holding up, Agnés?' Melissa began.

'Oh, I am fine.' Agnés smiled coyly at Arthur under her eyelashes.

'Do you go to many house parties with the Countess?' She must use this time wisely. The way things were going, who knew when she would get another chance.

'In the war we went all the time, nearly every weekend. It was exhausting, but now not so much. The Countess prefers the social whirl of London. That is good as she seldom wants me to accompany her in an evening.'

'Does she ever go home to France?'

'I am not sure.' Was that evasion? 'I have never been with her.'

'Never been? What, you mean you have never been to her estates?'

'Never, and I have not met her husband either.'

'How extraordinary, but you have been abroad with her elsewhere?' Here there might be some scope. Who knows who she had been hobnobbing with? Perhaps Agnés could supply them with a list.

'Oh, yes, she drags me around all over, but in Europe they are not so kind as you are. They see me and know I am just a poor relation. I am treated no more than a servant.'

'Absolute rotters,' exclaimed Arthur. 'How completely beastly for you. Come, my dear, let me give you a tour of the house.'

Infuriated with the interruption of her interrogation but seeing no way to prevent it, Melissa was left alone with the vicar and took this opportunity. 'Would now be a good time to have that chat?' She looked at the vicar – she hoped with an inviting look.

He glanced at Mrs Stokes. 'Perhaps not now.'

Taking the hint, Melissa said, 'Oh, Mrs Stokes, do you think you could rustle up a fresh pot of tea? No rush, though.' Quick on the uptake, Mrs Stokes removed the hideous teapot and left the room.

Melissa looked expectantly and encouragingly at the vicar. He looked decidedly uncomfortable. Quite a role reversal. He really was going to need some guidance if he was to fulfil his religious duties, she thought.

'This is very difficult for me, but I can tell you are a woman of the world, and if you accept the role at Pennstone we will be working together in the village, hopefully for many years to come. Listen, I am not … not what you would call a ladies' man. I find them a bit intimidating, to tell the truth. The victim of four elder sisters, formidable lot, three are missionaries.' He almost shuddered. 'Still, I digress. Some of the chaps in the army on leave felt they might have found a sympathetic soul. They they took me to a club, a private members' club …' His voice petered out.

'Yes?' Melissa encouraged. This didn't sound so bad.

What on earth was he going to reveal? Then, recalling her conversation with Maundeville and Alasdair, she began to get an inkling.

'A special club, if you get my drift. '

Melissa was beginning to. She schooled her face to remain open and bland, but her mind was working furiously. Was this what Maundeville and Alasdair were on about earlier? Not the vicar as well. What was it, an epidemic? How come she had never twigged this about men before now? Was this a disadvantage of her very expensive but private education? Not something the governesses covered, although the baron had been very forward-thinking in the education of a young girl, and she had been schooled well in mathematics and the sciences. If she had not met Alasdair, and there had not been an impending war, she would have considered attending university. Instead, it was used as an excuse by her mother for a finishing school, not in Switzerland, as planned – far too dangerous – but in the wilds of Yorkshire. Far too much fresh air and not enough cocktails for Melissa's liking at the time.

Something in her manner must have alerted him all the same, and his voice took on an even more cautious note. 'Not that I am, decidedly, that way at all. Please don't think that. It was a mistake. A genuine mistake, but one all the same.'

'It is of no concern to me, please be assured.' Melissa attempted a light touch. She was seriously intrigued now and anticipating revelations.

'Yes, well, you would be in a minority. I was horrified. These places are illegal. It is all illegal.' His voice had risen almost to a squeak. The vicar had gone very pink. He took out his handkerchief and wiped his brow. Melissa waited.

'Well, they are still God's creatures, and I felt that perhaps I could do some good. Bring them to God, if you will.'

Have it your way, Melissa thought sceptically. Then she wanted to slap her wrist. She was becoming appallingly cynical. The bishop would, however, sadly, be appalled. Or was he a man of the world as well?

'Anyway, I soon realised that it was not the sort of place I should be in. Especially as I had been offered my living here.' His vocal pitch lowered, approaching normal.

'But what does this have to do with George?' Melissa struggled to contain her exasperation.

'Nothing, per se. It was just a comment he made over the port on the first night.'

'Ah yes, I heard about that.' Bingo. Now it was coming.

'You did?' The vicar looked aghast.

'George could always be a spiteful cuz on occasion.'

'Yes, but it was more than that. You see, two other people round the table were also regularly at the club. I saw them. They saw me. I am sure.'

'Two?' She could not contain her shock.

'Yes, Bernard Lyon. I don't think he takes much trouble to hide his predilections to the observant. The Countess is clearly blind. Oh, pardon me, I didn't mean to …' He trailed off again. 'I really am so awfully sorry. I get so tongue-tied, quite the wrong turn of phrase, this is so difficult.'

'Who was the other?' Melissa asked quietly, slowly, clearly. Her nails bit into her palms as she was consumed with impatience. It was as much as she could do not to bounce around in anticipation.

'Godfrey Greenwood.

THIRTY-FIVE

It was as much as Melissa could do not to gasp out loud. Here was the evidence they sought – the link between Bernard Lyon and Godfrey Greenwood. The vicar was looking rather green after his revelations. Melissa's brain was threatening to go into overload. She needed to tell Maundeville as soon as she could. Should she telephone? No, too risky. She needed to get back to the house as soon as she could. This was a major breakthrough. Clearly not only was Greenwood a spy, but a murderer as well.

She stood up to conceal her excitement and trepidation from the vicar. She went over to the window and stood with her back to him, apparently gazing out at the formal garden. Night was falling; the sky was streaked with indigo, peach and red. Red sky at night, shepherd's delight, tripped into her mind. She smiled, and some of the tension dissipated. She heard the door open and turned. Mrs Stokes had returned with a fresh brew. Damping down her impatience, her good manners prevailed and she allowed Mrs Stokes to proffer her a fresh cup. She and the vicar sat there in silence, as if exhausted by their conversation. What more was there to say?

'Well, Arthur and Agnés have been a while, haven't

they? Hmm,' she ventured. 'I think the house has a rather nice Gainsborough in the dining room.'

'Really, I can't say as I have noticed. I must pay attention next time I am in there.' The vicar's tone bordered on maudlin.

'Do you think we have given them long enough?'

'Long enough for what?'

Melissa sighed. Hopeless, just hopeless. 'For their romancing, don't you know?'

'Oh.' The vicar flushed again, but this time he smiled. 'It would be jolly nice to have a wedding at All Saints'. It would be my first.'

The door opened, and Arthur and Agnés came back in. One look at their faces was enough to testify that all had gone well.

'Such a lovely house. So elegant. So stylish,' Agnés gushed. Arthur, eyes shining, chest puffed out, accepted the compliments with undisguised pleasure. Yes, an announcement was definitely in the offing. He had better be quick before the Countess took her away again. Melissa wondered if her aunt could be prevailed upon to offer her a temporary home until the wedding?

More tea was poured, dainty cakes consumed. Melissa was bursting to get on back to Pennstone, but she knew these things could not be rushed. She had undertaken to be a chaperone and that she would be. Mrs Stokes hovered, her eyes missing nothing.

'A fabulous ... what is it the English call it?... spread. That is it. Absolutely wonderful, Mrs Stokes. The pastries are so light, they melt in your mouth, my compliments,' Agnés said.

Mrs Stokes beamed at her housekeeping skills being so publicly and charmingly complimented. Agnés might be foreign, but clearly she would do.

'Well, I feel I have left Alasdair long enough,' Melissa hinted.

'Yes, yes, of course. You and the vicar start out and we will catch you up.'

Thus dismissed, Melissa waited with barely suppressed frustration as Stokes took his time returning their coats and hats. If the vicar was surprised at the speed she set on the return walk, he was too polite to mention it. They paused near the main entrance to Pennstone and Melissa took her leave. Loathe to get caught up in the greetings and inevitable exchange of pleasantries, she said, 'I think I'll just nip around the back. My shoes are so muddy.' She timed it just right so that the vicar was prevented from joining her as Smithers opened the door in anticipation of their arrival.

Ducking around the corner, Melissa spotted Rose crossing the courtyard; she seemed to be lugging a large kit bag with her and was making for the barn. Something in her furtive attitude attracted Melissa's attention and, forgetting all about Maundeville for that moment, Melissa turned and followed Rose. This could be a chance to talk to her alone. Though what on earth she was she doing out here in the dusk, she had no idea. It would be nigh on dark in the barn. With that in mind, she diverted and went into the scullery. There, on a hook, was an oil lamp with a box of matches conveniently placed beside it. She put her bag down and lit the lamp. Grabbing the handle, she left her bag and made her way over the yard once more. There was no sign of Rose now as darkness fell.

She slowly opened the door of the barn and, lifting the lamp high, stepped inside.

THIRTY-SIX

Alasdair let Davies lead him to the door of the barn. He was confident of his bearings now, and even if he fell over a stray bale of hay, his landing was pretty much guaranteed to be soft. He let Sheba off the lead and headed for her stall. He sat down on a bale, and after a few moments, she joined him, sitting at his feet, her muzzle resting on his knees. He felt around and found the brush Davies had mentioned and began to brush her. Preoccupied with his task, he almost missed the sound of the barn door opening. He stilled his hand and was about to call out. Perhaps this was Melissa looking for him, but something prescient stalled his voice. He stroked Sheba's muzzle to quieten her and listened.

Of course, a barn is never silent. The scurrying of the mice and rats as they went about their business created intermittent rustling, but at least in this barn, there was no horse to add to the background sound. This intruder was human, but as furtive as the rodents. He heard a click – the sound of a modern battery torch, he thought. Searching? Then there was a low distinctive cough, and suddenly he was back to the first night and the murder. Good God, he was here in the barn with the murderer and he couldn't see who it was!

The door creaked open again. More footsteps and the hiss of an oil lamp this time. 'You! I might have known. Always creeping around, watching, learning. I bet you were the school sneak.'

'I am sorry to disappoint you, Rose, but I never went to school.' It was Melissa's voice. She sounded strange, something in her voice. Excitement mixed with curiosity and fear?

'Well, lucky you. How do you think it feels to be teaching at the very school at which my parents spent a fortune educating me? And what was it all for? To catch a husband?'

'You don't have to let it be that way. You should be proud of your job. It is a real skill.'

Alasdair sat in the stall his mind racing. Rose? Rose? What did she have to do with all of this?

'Proud. Are you mad? It is my only respite from the constant drone of my mother. And what have I replaced it with? Spotty teenage girls who pity me – me! – for not being married. No engagement ring this holiday then, Miss? Can't you fence in a suitor, Miss? Lacrosse, Miss? Men don't like sporty girls do they, Miss?'

'So what is in the bag, Rose? It is a sports bag, isn't it?'

'Oh, yes. I shall need to get a new one now. It's all your fault.'

Good God, thought Alasdair, she sounds unhinged. A cold fear crept over him. That was Melissa out there. Had she thought to bring her gun?

'Mine? My fault? How do you deduce that?'

'Snooping around, interfering, asking questions. You made me do it. I had to silence her.'

'Do what?' Melissa sounded exasperated, not frightened now. Did she not realise the danger? Alasdair silently raged.

'Emma was going to ruin it all. She and her high and mighty principles. George was going to get the money. I could have made him marry me. I knew too much, he would have had to marry me, but then she interfered and had to be dealt with.'

'You?' Melissa sounded incredulous. 'You killed Emma? But why on earth did you do that? And what do you mean? Why was it my fault?'

Alasdair stood up, clasped Sheba's muzzle to keep her silent and crept towards the stall door. He prayed that the two women were too occupied with one another to hear him.

'You and your stupid aristocratic family, just like mine. I thought we Honourables should stick together, but George, he knew you too well. He said you would get all the money. That Lady Honor would never allow the Brigadier to give him and Emma their share no matter what he said. You have to understand. I had to marry him. I was desperate. This was my last chance. Don't you realise? Can't you see? Do you know nothing?' Rose's voice, harsh and guttural, was rising.

'And Meg, poor little Meg?'

'A servant, and a nosey one too. She got what she deserved. She listened in on me and Emma and then wanted to talk about it. To me, the Honourable Rose Tennant.'

'But if you wanted to marry George, why did you nearly kill him?'

'George? Oh, he suspected me. I am sure of it. He had been very odd with me since Emma died. I thought if he got the money off Bernard Lyon, we could get married quickly. And we would have been. Wait. What do you mean? Me? You think I hit him? What would be the point of that? I want a husband, not a corpse.'

'But, if you had waited, Brigadier Ferguson might have given you some money. In fact ...' Melissa stopped. What had she seen? The danger now, at last? This woman had just admitted to murder.

'I am tired of waiting, I want a husband now.'

There was a small crash as the torch hit the floor of the barn. It sounded like it had broken. Alasdair hoped so. Melissa seemed to be edging back towards the stall. Backwards, slowly, edging closer. There was a shuffling; he scuffed off his shoes.

'Ah. That is where the last silver carving knife went.' Melissa was clearly trying to keep her talking, playing for time. 'What else do you have in the bag, Rose?'

Another step, was she past the stall door?

'The bloody clothing. But you knew that didn't you, sneak? They've been looking for this all afternoon, haven't they? But I have been one step ahead.'

Alasdair could hear her voice near now, close, outside the stall door?

'Melissa, douse the light.' Alasdair commanded. There was a hiss.

'Ooh. The useless husband.' Then a wail. 'You idiots, it's pitch black in here now.'

Focusing on Rose's voice, Alasdair circled behind her. She was darting from side to side, still yelling obscenities.

He hoped she had the knife out in front of her. His strong left forearm encircled her neck, while the right struck her right arm, knocking the knife flying as he had intended. Swiping her legs from under her, he brought her down with his best school-rugby tackle. He pinioned her hands to her side by sitting on her and, using his knees, he used his freed right hand to extract the dog leash from his pocket. And now, pulling her hands behind her back, he secured them with the leash.

'Not so useless now,' Alasdair muttered in her ear.

THIRTY-SEVEN

'Iesu Mawr!' Davies arrived with another oil lamp. 'What the hell is going on here then?'

'Quick, Davies, fetch Maundeville and Thomas. We have our killer,' Alasdair yelled.

'What, that wee slip of a girl?'

'She may look a wee slip of a girl but as a games mistress she is all muscle. Quick, man. I can't sit here all day.'

Davies put the oil lamp down and left, his rubber gumboots slapping on the yard as he ran. Sheba had begun barking frantically. It all just added to the mayhem. Rose had been winded but was now shouting and cursing and attempting to roll over. When this failed to shift Alasdair, she tried screaming like a banshee.

Melissa got up from the floor of the barn where she had collapsed, her legs having given way in shock as it suddenly dawned on her how near to death she had come. She was furious. Fancy leaving her gun in the scullery. A good agent she was. Fear gave way to anger. A fury that threatened to overwhelm her. This woman had murdered two people and all because she wanted to marry George? It beggared belief. She stood there, fighting to control her temper, breathing slower, longer, feeling the anger dissipating.

"Recovered now?' Alasdair grinned in her direction.

He is bloody well loving this, Melissa thought. 'If you hadn't been here, I would be dead. You are amazing, incredible. Bloody hell,' she shouted over Sheba. She had to stop the dog barking. She went over to the stall, opened it and Sheba rushed out, still barking. She settled down on her haunches next to Alasdair in a perfect gundog pose; she stopped barking but growled steadily instead. At least it was quieter. Melissa moved to take her, but Alasdair said, 'No leave her. If the bitch moves, she'll bite her.' Melissa laughed, hilarity flooding in to replace the anger, and then stopped as hysteria threatened. She covered her mouth with her hand.

Rose stopped wailing and wriggling and attempted to turn her head to glare at the man sitting on her backside. He still looked very satisfied with his achievement. All he needed was a cigar to complete the picture.

Melissa was still attempting to squash the laughter. It was threatening to take over. Under control, she moved round to the front of Rose. She just could not believe it. This was the person that had killed her cousin Emma. Stabbed her? It was too incredible; they had discounted her as a suspect and yet here she was confessing.

'Did you really kill Emma?' Rose shifted under Alasdair; she looked at Melissa and gave no answer but just glared at her, baring her teeth. She looks deranged, Melissa thought. How on earth could we have predicted that? Giggles bubbled up again. Trust George, with all the choice in the country, to pick a madwoman. He really was a walking disaster. Then she thought of him, still lying in the hospital, and sobered. She was shaking now and, raising a trembling hand to her mouth, covered it in an attempt to regain her composure.

'My giddy aunt, just look at this, would you?' Maundeville had arrived. With him, was the constable.

'He should not be here.' Melissa gestured frantically at the constable. 'He should be with George. She didn't whack him,' Melissa shouted. 'George could still be in danger.'

'Bitch, bitch!' yelled Rose.

'He'll be safe for the moment. Shift, Alasdair. Well done, lad. Constable, help me get her up. We'll take her to the library.'

'Watch her, she has lost the plot. Absolutely barking,' Melissa warned. Looking at Sheba, she clamped her hand back over her mouth.

The constable yelled. Rose had attempted to bite him. He caught her arm roughly and hauled her out of the barn and across the yard, Rose screaming abuse at the constable all the way. Maundeville looked flustered. 'What the ...'

'Not going to go down quietly, is she?' Melissa took the lamp and began searching. 'The missing silver carving knife is here somewhere.'

'Don't touch it.' Maundeville produced a pristine white handkerchief. 'We'll get fingerprints off the handle if we are lucky.'

'There is also a kit bag around here somewhere. I think she was trying to hide it. Look here.'

Maundeville went over and unbuckled it. On opening the bag, he recoiled. Melissa could smell the rank smell of old blood from where she was standing. 'Well, you wouldn't have missed that this afternoon when searching. No wonder she wanted to hide it.'

With the blade of the knife held gingerly in the handkerchief and the kit bag in the other, Maundeville moved off, no doubt trying to catch up to the constable and his vociferous prisoner.

Now alone together in the barn, Melissa flung her arms around Alasdair's neck and proceeded to thank him thoroughly with a long, lingering kiss.

'Hmm, I must make a habit of saving your life. I like the reward.'

Melissa giggled genuinely now and then sobered. 'How could we have got it so wrong? She murdered Emma and Meg because she wanted to marry George? It is preposterous. Mad. Oh, and, of course, that means that the murders were in the family after all. Well, if George lives he has certainly had a narrow escape. Then who is the spy? What will happen now?'

Alasdair reached up and placed his fingers over her mouth. 'Shh, it is all right, breathe, be calm. There was absolutely no way any of us could have foreseen that we had a lunatic in our midst.'

He wrapped his arms around her and held her firmly as her breathing slowed and then she began to sob. Great heaving, wracking, cathartic sobs. When she stopped and was calm again, he released her slightly.

'I seem to be out of handkerchiefs and I think I'll need a fresh jacket.' He stroked her hair. 'Come on, darling, let's see what happens now.'

Melissa tucked Alasdair's hand under her elbow and prepared to follow Maundeville. 'What about Sheba?'

Her nose appeared to be attached to the back of Alasdair's knee. He put his hand out and caressed her ears.

'I think she has just been promoted to house dog, don't you?'

The three of them entered the house, through the scullery, up the servants' stairs and out into the main hall. They continued on and into the library. The constable and Davies were standing guard over Rose. She was sitting on a chair, her hands still tied behind her back.

Melissa found a chair for Alasdair, and Sheba lay herself down beneath it. Melissa remained standing, her hand resting lightly on Alasdair's shoulder. On the library table was the knife and the kit bag. Godfrey Greenwood was standing in the corner, pale and wide-eyed. Swiftly, Melissa went up to Maundeville and murmured in his ear, 'Get rid of Greenwood. I have information and so will she.' She rolled her eyes in Rose's direction.

Maundeville paused, blinked and then said, 'Greenwood, can you find Lady Honor and Brigadier Ferguson? Take them into the morning room and say that I'll be with them in a moment. Stay with them and keep them calm for me, will you? Order tea or something. We'll have to sort all this out first.' He waited for the door to close then rounded on Rose, 'Well, young lady. Just what have you done? And what do you know?'

'I am saying nothing. What's in it for me?' It was Rose's turn to laugh, low and insolent.

'No, sorry, Maundeville,' Alasdair interrupted, 'We have her, she has confessed in front of Melissa and I, but she says she did not attempt to kill George. We still have another potential killer out there and that has to do with the other matter. That is the urgent issue now.'

Maundeville frowned. 'Very well, we will do this your

way. Is there somewhere we can secure her until we are ready to question her?'

'Let me think … yes,' Melissa said. 'The new downstairs cloakroom. No window, a stout door and it can be locked from the outside.'

'Constable, take her there and bring the key back to me. No, pocket the key and guard the door. And you, young lady, I suggest you have a long hard think about what you have done and how you can help yourself.'

'Fat chance of that,' commented Melissa. 'I think she is a homicidal maniac.'

'And Greenwood. What is this information you have for us, Melissa?'

'It was the vicar, Harold James. He has supplied the link between Bernard Lyon and Godfrey Greenwood. They frequent the same club. A very specific club, if you catch my drift.'

'Phew.' He whistled. 'And we have been trying to find a connection between them. If this is true, Greenwood has covered it up well. Completely fooled the lot of us. Do you think the vicar will be a reliable witness? The Special Branch has really slipped up here. How on earth did they miss this? They were meant to be tailing the pair of them.'

'Hmm, not sure he will want to stick his head up above the parapet. Even by admitting he had been there, his career could be over. And that would be really unfair.'

'So what is the alternative?'

'Well, George is not dead yet, is he? He knew something like that. It explains his comment on the first night. Rose clearly lied about her conversation. Emma knew exactly what was going on and could possibly tie in the Countess as well, with any luck.'

'Quick! We have been overheard,' Alasdair called out. 'I just heard the click of the small library door.'

Melissa ran to the side door and flung it open, just as the main door to the small library shut. She ran across the room, Maundeville behind her. She could hear Alasdair yelling at her, 'Melissa, no, leave it to the experts.' She glanced behind her as she ran. But the only expert left was portly, middle-aged Maundeville, and he was already slowing.

They were in the main hall now, but it was empty. Where had the eavesdropper gone? The door to the morning room opened and Godfrey Greenwood appeared. 'What is going on? I heard shouting.'

'It's fine, go back in there,' Maundeville shouted between gasps.

'No, I think not.' Greenwood ran across the tiled floor, skidding in front of the staircase and took those two at a time. Turning left at the top, Melissa could not say quite why she followed him. It just seemed the right thing to do. But he was a fit young man, and by the time she got to the guest wing, he had disappeared. Maundeville came panting up behind her.

'Which is his room?' she asked.

Maundeville pushed past. 'Up here at the end.' He led the way now, down the corridor. He tried the door. It was locked. He took a short run at it, hitting it with his shoulder, but he did not have the enough strength. The door was a solid Victorian oak.

Melissa ran back up the corridor and leant over the

banisters. 'Henry? Constable? Brigadier? We need help, quick, quick,' she shrieked. Gosh, I sound like Rose, she thought.

Within minutes, Henry Blake and the constable were attempting to force the door open. Brigadier Ferguson. They had called for Smithers in case there was another key.

At last, the lock on the door gave way, ripping out of the door frame without warning, catapulting Henry Blake into the room first. Melissa peered over his shoulder. The constable attempted to push him aside. Henry got there first.

Godfrey Greenwood was lying across the bed, unconscious. Dead? Henry dropped to his knees, lifted one of Greenwood's arms, feeling at the wrist for a pulse. He sniffed.

'Bitter almonds,' Henry said. 'Potassium cyanide. He's dead. A spy's way out.'

THIRTY-EIGHT

By some sort of common assent, the family all congregated in the blue drawing room. Brigadier Ferguson had sent Smithers for some drinks. Looking at her wristlet watch, Melissa realised that it was now six thirty in the evening. Dinner would be late, if at all, tonight.

'Is it over?' she asked Alasdair in a whisper.

'All bar the shouting. And there will be some if Rose is anything to go by.'

'But who was listening in?'

'Lady Honor, who was in the morning room with you before all the drama?' Alasdair asked. He had no such scruples. Now was the time for it all to come out in the open.

'Well, we were instructed to go there by Godfrey Greenwood, and he joined us and then the Countess came in ...'

'The Countess, was it? Listening at the door of the library?' Melissa was still trying to grasp just what had happened and which pieces of the jigsaw of events fitted where.

'It makes sense. She was warning Greenwood his cover was blown.'

'Did you hear anything they were saying?' Melissa asked.

Brigadier Ferguson shook his head. ''Fraid I was not paying any attention. There has still been no news from the hospital.'

'And you, Lady Honor?'

'No, I am afraid not, they were talking in very low voices. I thought it might be in her own language but then she is French, isn't she? And it wasn't French. I would have recognised that.'

'Could it have been German?' Alasdair persisted.

Mandeville shook his head at that and then, remembering, said, 'No point leading the witness, Alasdair.'

'I am most frightfully sorry, but I just could not say what language it was,' Lady Honor stated firmly.

Melissa almost ground her teeth; she could see her frustration mirrored in Alasdair's face.

'But you think it was her listening at the door?' Maundeville speculated.

'Looks like it,' Alasdair said morosely. 'But we will never prove it now Greenwood is, conveniently, dead.'

'Well, less mess to clear up, but I am going to have a hell of a job explaining this to the prime minister.'

'Where is the Countess now?' Melissa could not let it go. This was not how she had imagined it would end. She had thought all the ends would be tied up neatly and all would be revealed. Had Greenwood acted on his own? How were the Countess and Bernard Lyon implicated? Had the link been stopped at the Secret Intelligence Service? How would they now find out what had happened to Alasdair and who attacked him? It was all too much for her to assimilate. She sat down on the couch abruptly and put her face in her hands, rubbing her face as if to remove the film of dirt and subterfuge that had settled there.

Maundeville looked around vaguely. Now it seemed to be all over, he appeared to have lost interest or focus. Melissa was confused. Why did he not take charge?

'The Countess and Bernard Lyon are in the green drawing room,' Lottie replied. She was clutching Henry Blake's hand as if she would never let go.

'Should we separate them? Aren't we giving them time to concoct a story?' Melissa persisted, trying to force Maundeville into action. She felt Alasdair's hand on her arm. He had found her, and his strength gave her courage.

'What difference does it make?' Maundeville snapped. 'We needed proof and now we have none. Still, at least the mole in the service has been exposed.'

'You hope,' muttered Henry Blake.

'You can't print that!' Maundeville warned. Then he smiled a sly smile, 'You could, of course, interview the Countess and Bernard Lyon for an exclusive. It would be interesting to hear just what they have concocted. Eh, what?'

Henry looked at Lottie and she gave a shrug, and then a smile. They left the room with an alacrity that made Melissa grin. Henry would get his scoop, and it looked like Lottie would get her man.

'We are going to have to unpick that charity and be damned with the consequences,' Maundeville muttered gloomily.

'When is Special Branch arriving?' Alasdair asked.

'No idea, they should be here soon.' Mandeville sighed. 'Well, we might as well question the girl now. You never know she might be prepared to help us. Give us some insight into just what Emma was caught up in.'

'I wouldn't bank on it,' Melissa muttered to Alasdair. 'I don't think homicidal lunatics co-operate, do you?'

The constable was sent off once again to fetch Rose. She still looked truculent while somehow maintaining an air of affected boredom. The perfect aristocrat.

'Well, young lady. Now you have had time to cool your heels, what do you have to tell us?'

'Get knotted. Lady is the correct term. I am the Honourable Rose Tennant and you have absolutely no jurisdiction over me.'

'No, but I do,' came a fresh voice. Melissa had been so intent on observing Rose that she had not even registered him entering the room. 'Superintendent Melrose, Special Branch.'

Rose eyed the tall, commanding uniformed officer with disdain. 'I have nothing to say, and I want to speak to my father, Lord Treggwent.'

Melissa could contain herself no longer. 'But she knows. She murdered Emma because Emma found out about the stupid plan to touch up Bernard Lyon for money and objected. I bet it was her idea. Whatever else George is, he is not a blackmailer. Whereas she … she killed Meg too.'

'But I needed him for money.' Rose sounded calm, even reasonable now. 'George, I mean. My parents wouldn't accept him otherwise. And the stupid servant just got in the way.'

'But if you had just waited, Brigadier Ferguson ...'

'How was I to know? George didn't believe it would ever happen. Your stupid cousin Lottie was full of it. How you were the favourite niece. How you were bound to inherit it all and she wouldn't be able to marry Henry. You have no idea. You who are already married! Selfish bitch!' Her tirade ended in a shriek.

Glancing around the room, Melissa saw that the men looked positively aghast. All except Superintendent Melrose; he maintained an enviable sangfroid in the face of this utter madness. She was appalled herself. How could she have got it so wrong? How could she and Alasdair not have seen that Rose was a lunatic? Not suspected something? Anything? She felt so stupid, and yet how could they have known?

'Give her the phone call, now,' Melrose said, his calm deep voice cutting some order into the tension of the room.

The constable then put his hand on her arm to guide her over to the desk, on which was the phone.

'Take your hand off me, you swine,' she said, calm once more. Then, Rose serenely walked up to the phone. Then there ensued an interesting one-way conversation in which Rose informed her father of her predicament. When she had put the phone down, she howled with laughter. 'Well, what fun. My father is going to engage your father, Charters. Do you think he'll take the case?'

EPILOGUE

I t had been a fine day for the wedding. The bride looked exquisitely happy. The groom was beaming with pride as they shook hands with well-wishers outside All Saints' Church.

Melissa, watching them with Alasdair's arm tucked through hers, basked in the reflection of their combined happiness. It had been a hard few months. There were relatively few guests. They had both wanted it low key, but the church had nevertheless been packed with the villagers, come to wish them well or just to gawp.

Looking at a small group standing to the right of the happy couple, she took Alasdair over to them. Lottie looked bright and happy. She threw her arms around them both and then stood back and waggled her left hand at them. On it was a discreet engagement ring. Melissa glanced at Henry, resplendent in his morning suit: new, Savile Row, she thought. He shrugged as if to say what could I do? Melissa had read several of his by-lines in The Times to Alasdair in recent months, so she hoped he was doing well. It would be good for them to catch up at the reception.

Then, with slightly glistening eyes, she turned and gave

George a huge hug and held it longer than necessary. He returned it and gave her a chaste peck on the cheek. He had arrived in an enormous, flashy motor; she wondered whom he had earmarked for the sale. The groom, she suspected.

She wondered, fleetingly, how Rose was doing. She never came to trial. She had been declared unfit to plead and presently was locked up in an expensive and luxurious asylum for the aristocratic criminally insane.

She sighed. Emma, poor Emma. She would have loved to have been here. To see a refugee, no matter that she was an aristocrat, dear Agnés, marrying their neighbour, Arthur, would have given her such a thrill. Still, she had done some good. The charity had been wound up, the titled sponsors claiming they had been duped had quietly slipped away into the shadows to lie low until everything had blown over.

Bernard Lyon was apparently now in the United States, keeping his head down, making money. The Countess, well, she had drifted back into her fast set, still pleading innocence. She had engaged a maid since she had lost her companion and spent much of her time on the continent.

Alasdair had spent some time with Special Branch and Maundeville in Whitehall, unpicking everything Greenwood had done while employed by the SIS. He had covered his tracks well. A few names had been unearthed; a couple of clerks had been discreetly put under surveillance. He had been an excellent operative, his motivation unknown, beyond that threat of blackmail. His English family had been horrified and had co-operated fully. It was clear they were not involved beyond unwittingly giving him a home and an impeccable background. The German Secret Service were playing a long game, one that they would have to monitor closely. However, Melissa was pleased when Alasdair walked away and returned with her to Pennstone Manor and began the renovations and work on the farm that was needed. He seemed resigned and made peace with the fact that he might never know what happened in that dark church in France.

Melissa straightened her shoulders; this was not the occasion for such thoughts. Time enough for the reckoning that was coming. One day, she vowed, she would find out, and if the Countess was involved, she had better look out. Alasdair may have turned a corner over the last few months – the investigation had given him a purpose – but there was a bruise on their life, its livid colours taking time to fade. But not today.

She turned to her family and said, in reminiscence of their childhood, 'Come on, you slow coaches, last one to the champagne is a sissy.'

ACKNOWLEDGEMENTS

I would like to thank Consuelo Rivera-Fuentes and Sophie Lloyd-Owen from Victorina Press for giving me the opportunity to be published.

Special thanks to Katherine Trail, my copy editor, whose eagle eyes and sensitive suggestions improved the final edit.

To my editor Jill French for her expertise and getting the book up to standard for submission.

Also to Heidi Hurst for the wonderful layout and typesetting. It looks wonderful!

To my initial readers and their valuable comments from their wealth of experience, Tracy Baines and Judy Hall

Special thanks to Village Writers in the New Forest who have helped me on my journey over the past five years, especially Sue and Mike our splendid hosts. A special mention to the late Mario Reading who was so generous with his time and intelligent feedback to us all, fledgling authors as well as the more experienced and published.

I thought I knew enough about the Golden Age of Crime fiction, but thanks must go to Martin Edwards through his blog and books *The Golden Age of Murder* and *The Story of Classic Crime in 100 books*, that showed me how much more there was to appreciate and learn.

Finally, to public libraries, especially those in Bournemouth, where all my research began with books I could never have afforded myself. May you last for ever.

ABOUT THE AUTHOR

Vicki worked as a Chartered Librarian for the Royal National Institute of Blind People and then for the past 19 years in public libraries in Bournemouth and Poole. There she enjoyed arranging and attending writing courses and author events, including such luminaries as Fay Weldon and Peter James.

All the while she was writing away in her spare time. She is intensely grateful to Village Writers based in the

New Forest who let her join them four years ago and have nurtured and critiqued her debut novel *Blind Witness* on its way to publication.

Born in California but brought up in England she was introduced to the Golden Age of crime authors at an early age by her mother.

She is married to a blind physiotherapist, and it is from his mother, born in a large country house in Devon (now a hotel), educated by governess and with a cut glass voice like the Queen, that she absorbed real life stories about the twenties and thirties.

She has always had a fascination with the Art Deco period and the Golden Age of crime writing. She has been filling her house with Art Deco inspired artefacts and clothing for 40 years.

Blind Witness is her debut novel and is the beginning of a series featuring Alasdair and Melissa Charters.

OTHER BOOKS BY VICTORINA PRESS

Desentrañando Memorias *** *Unravelling Memories* (2017)
edited by Consuelo Rivera-Fuentes
> (Bilingual anthology of poetry with Latin-American poets resident in the UK)

My Beautiful Imperial by Rhiannon Lewis (2017)
> (Historical fiction; recommended by the Walter Scott Prize Academy)

The Marsh People by M.Valentine Williams (2018)
> (Dystopian, science-fiction novel for young adults and adults at heart)

Blind Witness by Vicki Goldie (2018)
> (Murder mystery novel, first book in The Charters' Murder Mysteries Series)

The Secret Letters From X to A by Nasrin Parvaz (2018)
> (Historical fiction set in Iran's Joint Committee Interrogation Centre where the author spent 8 years as a political prisoner)

Violeta Walks on Foreign Lands *** *Violeta Anda en Tierras Extrañas* (2018) edited by Odette Magnet & Consuelo Rivera-Fuentes

(Bilingual short stories by Latin-American and Spanish writers inspired by the life and work of Chilean singer, songwriter, painter and ceramicist Violeta Parra).

FORTHCOMING TITLES:

A Woman's Struggle in Iran: A prison Memoir by Nasrin Parvaz (December 2018)

(The haunting memoir of the author's 8 years in an Iranian prison).

The Bomb on the Winnipeg by Adam Feinstein (2019)

(A gripping novel of passion, poetry, pride and searing jealousies and betrayals – but above all, an exceptionally exciting thriller).

The Ardent Witness by Danielle Maisano (2019)

(A novel about an American woman trying to make sense of the chaos in her life through poetry, art and travels).